A Thug's Romance for Valentine's Day

A novel by Lady Lissa

Copyright © 2020 Lady Lissa
Published by Unique Pen Publications, LLC
All rights reserved. No part of this book may be reproduced in any form without written consent of the publisher, except brief quotes used in reviews.
This is a work of fiction. Any references or similarities to actual events, real people, living or dead, or to real locals are intended to give the novel a sense of reality. Any similarity in other names, characters, places, and incidents are entirely coincidental.

Prologue

Alissa

Valentine's Day 2018

I couldn't wait for Maverick to get home from his business trip. He had been gone for the past week and I had missed him so much. I was planning something special for him tonight. I felt like he needed this special dinner to welcome him home. He couldn't have come home at a better time… after all, today was Valentine's Day. I had hoped that he would've sent me some flowers or something, but he hadn't. All day I had patiently waited, but nothing came.

I'd be lying if I said I wasn't a little bit in my feelings about that. All the other women in the office received red roses except me and those who were single. It really put me in a weird place because this was the most romantic day of the year and my man hadn't sent me anything. I waved it off as him planning something big for tonight. I figured he was preparing to catch his flight back today and that he would have something for me later. At least that was my hope.

I hoped he hadn't forgotten today was Valentine's Day.

When I got off work at five o'clock, I made my way to the grocery store to pick up the ingredients that I'd need for dinner. I planned to smother some beef steaks in onions, peppers and mushrooms. I was going to bake some potatoes and smother them in butter, bacon and shredded cheddar cheese. I was also going to cook some rice and French cut green beans like my granny used to make for Sunday dinner. I was going to stop and pick up a strawberry covered cheesecake from the Cheesecake Factory for dessert. I couldn't wait for tonight.

My ringing phone drew me from my romantic thoughts about my man. I looked at the dashboard and saw my sister's name on the screen. I immediately connected the call.

"Hey Shelby, whatchu up to?" I asked.

"Girl fighting this damn traffic to get home. What about you?"

"The same, but I'm on my way to H.E.B. on Westheimer."

"What are you going do there?"

"Get the stuff I need to cook dinner for me and Maverick. He's coming home tonight," I beamed happily.

"Oh, that's right. I almost forgot he was coming back today. What are you cooking?"

"I'm gonna smother some steak, with rice and granny's beans, and baked potatoes on the side."

"Mmmm! Sounds delicious! Save a plate for me," she said.

"Girl bye! I'm sure you and Delaney have big plans for tonight," I said.

"Well, he did say he was taking me out to dinner. I'm not sure where yet, but I'm excited to see what he got me."

"Maybe he'll finally propose," I said.

"I don't know. We've only been dating a couple of years..."

"A couple of years is enough time to know if you want to spend the rest of your life with someone or not. You and Delaney are so in love. I just know he wants to marry you."

"Maybe, but if not, I wouldn't be disappointed. I'm not in any rush."

I pulled into the parking lot and found a parking spot. Once I did that, I quickly ended the call with my sister promising to call her tomorrow so we could exchange details about our night.

I had tried calling Maverick before I got out of the car, but he didn't answer. I just smiled because that had to mean he was on the plane heading back this way. I couldn't stop smiling as I walked in H.E.B. pushing my cart. I walked around the crowded veggie section collecting the ones I needed. Then I made my way to the butcher's area because I wanted my steaks to be fresh.

Once I got what I needed, I continued down the aisles picking up everything I needed. I wanted tonight to be so special for my man. I planned a nice romantic dinner by candlelight before we exchanged gifts. I was anxious to see what he got me. I knew it couldn't possibly be a ring because we had only been dating six months. I hoped it was a nice piece of jewelry though. I loved jewelry, especially diamonds and rubies.

I was down the gravy aisle when I heard a familiar voice on the next aisle. Even though I knew it sounded a lot like his voice, I couldn't believe it was him. I knew I had to be mistaken.

"I'm so glad to finally be back home," said the female voice.

"So, you didn't have fun in the Caribbean?" I heard the male voice asked.

"Hell yea, I had fun baby! Who wouldn't have fun on their honeymoon surrounded by beautiful crystal blue water?" she giggled as I heard them kiss.

"I'm glad you had fun babe. I know I definitely enjoyed myself witcho fine ass!" he said.

My ears had to be playing tricks on me. There was no way that this chick said she was on a honeymoon with who I thought it was. I grabbed my purse, left the cart and made a beeline for the next aisle. Something wasn't right and I had to find out if it was who it sounded like on that aisle. As I rounded the corner, I didn't see the two people who were just chatting a couple of seconds ago. I had to find out where they were. I quickly brushed pass a couple of shoppers in my haste to find the pair. As I rounded the left corner, I saw a man and woman kissing halfway down the aisle.

From behind, I could tell that the guy standing in front of me and kissing some woman I didn't know was Maverick. Tears began to fall from my eyes as I stood glued to my spot. My heart picked up the pace making me feel like I was about to have a heart attack. I couldn't believe my eyes. He said he was on a business trip for the past six days. The woman he was kissing said they had been on a honeymoon. Had he really married that woman behind my back? There was only one way to find that out and that was to make my feet move towards them and ask. I took a deep breath and prepared myself for what was sure to be a showdown. Either I was going to kick someone's ass and go to jail or get my ass jumped and end up in the hospital. One thing was for certain and that was I wasn't leaving here without an explanation.

Chapter one

Alissa

With every step I took, my hands and knees shook more and more. I couldn't believe that I was in this store getting groceries for a candlelight dinner with a man who wasn't even mine anymore. I wanted to scream and shout. I wanted to grab one of those bottles off the shelf and knock him behind the head.

The closer I got to the two of them, the madder I became. I walked behind him and pushed him as hard as I could. He stumbled against the shopping cart with full force. Shit, I might be small, but I packed a punch and he deserved it.

"Ayyo, what the fuck bruh?!" Maverick said as he turned to face me. The look on his face when he saw me was one of surprise and shame. Then that look turned into one of a dog begging to be let out. He had that look in his eyes that was pleading with me to not make a scene and when he saw that was exactly what I planned to do, he rolled his eyes and ran his hand down his face. "Aw shit!"

"Aw shit?! Is that all you got to say to me Maverick? Is this what the hell you doing Maverick? Huh?" I asked as I stared at him angrily in the face. "I thought you were coming home today to spend Valentine's Day with me and this is what you're doing!"

The pain that I was feeling right now was equivalent to the pain I felt when my grandmother passed last year. I felt sweaty and hot. My chest hurt probably because my heart was breaking. My mouth was so dry it felt like the Sahara Desert. I thought this man loved me. I really thought he was the one. I had allowed myself to believe that he was the one, and now look at him. Standing there with his arm around some other bitch looking as if he had seen a ghost.

"Who the fuck is this bitch Maverick?!" the woman asked with anger written on her face.

"Bitch? Who the hell you calling a bitch?" I asked. "You don't fucking know me!"

"I'm calling you a bitch for putting your hands on my husband!" she said.

"Your husband?! So, you married now Maverick? You're married?!"

"You damn right he's married!" She said as she shoved the huge rock and diamond wedding band in my face. I immediately looked at Maverick's left hand to find a ring on his ring finger also.

As dry as my mouth was, I wasn't done with this fool yet. How could he have been cheating on me with this bitch? Why didn't I know he had a wife?

"Maverick you're married?" I asked.

"I already told you he's married!" the woman said.

"I didn't ask you shit! Answer me Maverick!" I yelled angrily.

He stood there with his mouth hanging open, but no words were coming out. "Babe who is this woman? I'ma need you to say something because I'm about to punch her ass!"

"Bitch I wish you would..."

"Call me a bitch again and I'ma show you!" she said as she lunged for me. Maverick quickly jumped in front of her to stop her.

"Babe stop! We just got back from our honeymoon. Ain't nobody trying to be going down to the jailhouse to bail you out," he said to her.

"Honeymoon? You told me you were on a business trip!" I said.

"Maverick, you really need to say something because I'm two seconds from coming out of my lady character. Who the fuck is she?" the woman asked as she glared at me.

"That's the chick I told you I broke up with..."

"Broke up with? When did we break up Maverick? Huh? Huh?!" I asked as I glared at him. I was totally confused. "You were just in my fucking bed two weeks ago!" Now, he looked like a deer caught in headlights. He was trying to claim a breakup to save faith with this bitch. Aw hell no!

"Girl get the fuck out my face with all that bullshit and lies! This is my wife! You got it? She's my wife! Anything you think that we had is done!" Maverick said as he looked at me with anger filled eyes.

Who is this man? Why is he speaking to me like this? He's never spoken to me like this before!

My insides were quivering and my hand was itching to touch somebody. However, the last thing I wanted was to end up in jail behind some mess with a lying, cheating scumbag like Maverick James. I wanted so badly to break down and cry, but I wasn't going to do it. Not in front of this nigga or his bitch, and certainly not in front of all these damn people. Our little scene in the grocery store had started to draw a crowd. What I needed to do was save the little bit of dignity I still had. So, instead of breaking down and screaming while crying my eyes out in front of these total strangers, I decided to do what I should've done as soon as I saw his ass.

WHAP!

"DON'T YOU EVER COME NEAR ME AGAIN!!" I said as I pointed my finger in his face.

The girl quickly smacked my hand away. "Bitch I done told you to keep your hands off my husband!"

I was about to jump on her ass, but then I noticed all the phones that were out recording us. I just ran out of the store as quickly as I could. As I was making my way out of the store, I bumped into someone. I didn't know who it was, but he smelled really good. He held on to me so I wouldn't fall, but after what I had just been through, I didn't want his damn hands on me.

"Get your fucking hands off me!" I said as I started swatting his hands away from any parts of me.

"Aye, you bumped into me!" he said with an attitude.

"I don't give a fuck! Get your hands off me!" I repeated.

He released me and said, "Fine! I should've let yo fuckin' ungrateful ass fall!"

I looked up and into his handsome face. "Yea, I guess you should've!" I said before I took off running again.

Fuck him! Who asked for his damn help anyway?

I couldn't get to my car fast enough, especially not after that embarrassing moment. I mean, first that shit with Maverick, then with that asshole. As soon as I got to my car, I unlocked the door and slid into the driver's seat. I immediately broke down crying profusely. I couldn't believe that shit had happened to me. I couldn't believe that Maverick had done me that way. In front of a store full of strangers, he made me look like a fucking fool. What kind of Valentine's Day was that?

It was the worse Valentine's Day of my life. That's what it was. From here on out, fuck Valentine's Day! Fuck love!

I was sitting in my car in the parking lot crying my eyes out when I heard someone tapping on my glass. Who the fuck was that? I looked up and saw the dude I had bumped into holding my phone in his hand. I guess I must have dropped it when I collided into him. I rolled my window down and took the phone.

"Thank you," I said.

"No problem. You aight?" he asked.

"What do you care?"

"You really don't have to cop an attitude. I just wanted to return your phone. Now that I see you're upset I'm just trying to make sure you straight."

"Why?" I asked.

"I'on know. Shit, you ran out of there so fast and had such an attitude. I don't know who shit in your cornflakes this morning, but we don't all do that shit. Some of us like our cornflakes with milk," he said.

That shit was confusing to me, but it made me laugh.

"What? Is that a smile?"

I continued to smile and blush like a high school girl with a crush. I had almost forgotten what had just gone down inside the store until Maverick and his bitch walked out. I guess the tense look on my face gave the dude a reason to look in the direction my eyes were locked on.

My blood was literally boiling at this point. On Valentine's Day, this nigga had not only stood me up but had gotten married too. "Thanks for my phone," I said.

I rolled up my window and peeled out of the parking lot, leaving the dude standing there looking at me confused in my rearview window. I had to get out of there as quickly as possible because I was tempted to run over that nigga and his bitch. I couldn't believe this shit was happening to me. What had I done wrong?

I fucked that nigga like my life depended on it every time we were together. I cooked, cleaned and washed his dirty drawls too. Why wasn't I good enough for him? Why wasn't I enough for him?

As if she could sense that I needed her, Shelby started ringing my phone. I didn't want to speak to my sister or anyone right now, but I had to speak to somebody. Maverick had done me so wrong and I felt like I was about to explode. Maybe talking to my sister would help me get past all this shit that I was feeling.

"Hello," I answered, barely able to speak. I grabbed a Burger King napkin from the glove box and wiped my tears.

"What's wrong? What happened?"

"Everything is a mess!" I cried.

"Where are you?" she asked in a panic.

"I'm on my way home."

"I'll meet you there!"

"Okay."

I ended the call and dried my eyes again so I could make my way home through this traffic. I hated that Maverick had done that to me. He acted like he didn't care that he had hurt my feelings. Of all the days he could've done that to me, he picked the most romantic day of the fucking year. My gas light came on, so I pulled into the Chevron parking lot to put gas. I was going to use my debit card at the pump but changed my mind. I wasn't about to let any credit card skimmer get my damn numbers so they could wipe out my account.

I walked into the gas station and towards the glass cooler where the drinks were kept. I grabbed a bottle of chilled Sutter Home wine and headed to the register. I walked up to the cashier and put the bottle on the counter. "I'd also like 20 on pump six please," I said as I sniffled.

"28.89," he said.

I swiped my debit card while he bagged the wine I purchased. He gave me a receipt and the wine, and I headed for the exit. I pushed the door open and BAM!

"Yo ma…" the dude said.

I looked up and it was the same dude I bumped into earlier when I was leaving the grocery store. Could this day get any worse?

"Damn! Are you following me or something?" I asked with an attitude.

"Following you? What the fuck I got to be following you for?" he asked with an equally nasty attitude.

As he tried to walk around me to go inside the store, I stopped him. "Uh, are you gonna replace that?" I asked, referring to my wine bottle that now lay in pieces at my feet.

"Replace what? You bumped into me once again not paying attention to where you were going!"

"No, I didn't! I pushed the door open…"

"Yea, right into my fuckin' gut! You lucky I ain't pressing charges on your ass!" he said.

"Pressing charges?!" I asked as I pressed my hand to my chest.

One of the gas station attendants excused the two of us as she busied herself trying to clean up the mess of glass and wine. The dude took that moment to head inside the store. Shit, if he thought that was the end of this conversation, he was sadly mistaken. I followed him in and watched as he headed for the restroom. I walked to the coolers and grabbed another bottle of wine. I waited near the restroom door so when he would come out, he would see my ass waiting. He pushed the restroom door open and looked down at my small 5'3 frame.

"Tuh!" he commented as he walked to the coolers.

"Tuh my ass! You are going to pay for my bottle of wine that you destroyed!" I said as I followed behind him.

"Look lady, I don't have time for this shit! You need to pay me for my dry cleaning for spilling that shit on my damn pants and shoes!" he remarked.

He grabbed a blue Powerade and headed to the register. He placed his bottle on the counter and I placed mine as well. The cashier looked at him and asked, "Will this be together or separate?"

"Separate!" he said.

"TOGETHER!!" I commented.

The cashier was confused, but I wasn't. This man had bumped into me twice today. He wasn't about to just walk away from me without paying for my damn wine! I was just tired of men trying to play me because I was small. Not to say that I was sure that was the reason, but shit, what else could it be. I was 5'3 while he stood well over six feet. It hurt my damn neck to look up at this man, but I wasn't backing down.

A novel by Lady Lissa

Chapter two

Malik aka Bishop

This lil chick clearly had me mistaken for someone else. When she bumped into me coming out of H.E.B., she seemed quite a bit upset. That was verified when I went to bring her phone to her which she had dropped upon our collision. When I saw the way that she was staring at the dude with some chick in the parking lot, I really thought she was thinking about running both of them over. I hoped she wouldn't do something like that though and thank God she didn't. Thank God she had the good sense that he gave her to roll out. My guess was that he used to be her boyfriend or was her boyfriend until she caught him with the woman he was with.

I went inside H.E.B., grabbed what I needed and headed out. I had to stop for gas on the way home, so I pulled into the parking lot of the Chevron gas station since it was the closest and parked my ride next to pump seven. I chirped the alarm once I got out and headed inside. As I was about to pull the door open, I found it being pushed towards me. You could imagine how I felt in that moment seeing as how it was the second time today that someone had bumped the shit out of me.

I knew I wasn't losing weight or anything. I was 6'2 and weighed 200 pounds, so I knew darn well I was big enough for anyone to see me. You can imagine my surprise when I saw the same chick that bumped into me not that long ago in H.E.B. The bottle she was holding slipped from her hand and crashed on the concrete. I was livid when the shit splashed on my brand- new J's and pants. The exchange between us after that wasn't too pleasant.

This lil chick was mad as fuck... talking about I had better replace her wine. She bumped into me with that damn door. She pushed my ass with that door. Why the fuck did I need to replace the wine that slipped from her hand? Shit, she probably wasn't even old enough to drink in the first place. That was neither here nor there because what I didn't have time for was to keep arguing with her. I had shit to get done.

I bypassed her little short ass and headed to the restroom to wipe my fucking shoes off. That shit pissed me off because I had paid almost three hundred for these shoes. I cleaned the wine off them as best I could then walked out of the restroom to find her standing there waiting for me. She must have lost her damn mind.

I walked up to the counter and placed my Powerade on it. She put her wine on the counter next to my Powerade. The confused look on the cashier's face was probably like looking in a mirror. "Will this be together or separate?" he asked.

"Separate!" I said.

"TOGETHER!!" she shouted angrily.

I turned to look at her as she glared up at me with a hand on her hip. I looked at the cashier who had an amused look on his face at this point. Considering we were holding up the line, I decided to pay for her shit. Better that than to have her make an even bigger scene than before. I pushed the wine towards the dude and said, "You can ring them up together. I also need 30 on pump seven."

He rung up the items and gave me a total. I pulled the wad of cash out of my pocket and handed him a 50. He handed me the change and I grabbed my Powerade and headed for the door. Since she was behind me, I thought it would be rude of me to go out the door before her, so I held it open and allowed her to pass through first.

"Thanks," she said.

I watched as her short frame walked towards her car, a 2018 Jeep Grand Cherokee. She was fine even though she was shorter than I was. She was just petite but had a nice little rump. She must have weighed no more than a buck and a quarter. Her hair was curly and a little past her shoulders and her caramel skin seemed to glisten in the sun... like she had put some kind of shimmery sunscreen on. She was beautiful, but feisty as fuck. She had way too much attitude.

I watched as she placed the bottle of wine and her purse in the car before she started pumping the gas. It was like fate was pushing us together seeing as how her car was right next to my truck. I placed the Powerade on the hood of my truck and started pumping gas.

"You know you're really a beautiful girl. You should try smiling sometimes," I said.

She looked at me with somber eyes. They were red and puffy from all the crying she had been doing. "Leave me alone please," she said.

"That right there is your problem! Your attitude and that chip on your shoulder!"

"You don't know shit about me, so stop acting like you do!"

"I know somebody hurt your feelings, so now you think all men are the same," I said.

"Please don't judge me. Just pump your gas and let me be!"

"You could at least say thanks for the wine," I said.

She looked at me with a smirk on her face. "Wow! You really are full of yourself!"

"I'm full of myself because I expect a thank you for doing something nice for you. I didn't have to buy you that wine," I remarked.

"You made me drop the one I had bought so yes, you needed to buy me another bottle!"

"We obviously remember things differently, so I'll let you slide."

I stood there pumping the gas while stroking my goatee. "Let me slide my ass!" she said as she put the nozzle in the cradle and closed her gas tank. "You know what? You are way too good looking to be such an ass!"

With that being said and before I could respond, she slid in the driver's seat and rode out. I didn't know who she was or if I'd ever see her again, but she had definitely left an impression on me. I smiled as I finished pumping the gas in my truck. As I replaced the nozzle, I almost forgot about my Powerade.

I hopped in my burgundy GMC Yukon with black rims and dark tint and headed to the spot to check on my dudes. I ran the northside of H-Town from Acres Homes to Rankin and I had four trap houses around the city. Keys was my right- hand man and there was no one I trusted more than him. He and Tony Shivers were the only ones I kept in charge while I was away from the scene.

It was funny how as I drove towards the northside, I couldn't get that chick off my mind. She was real pretty, but that attitude. I wasn't sure why she was crying earlier, but I was more than sure she had gotten dumped by the dude I saw in the parking lot. As I drove, my phone started ringing. I picked it up because I saw that it was my baby mama, Priscilla.

"Hello," I answered.

"What are you doing Malik?"

"Why you asking? Whatchu need?"

"Uh, you were supposed to be coming to watch the kids for me to go to the casino with Kiki and Bailey."

I checked the time on the dashboard and saw that it was only six o'clock. I didn't know why she was rushing me to hang with those bitches. They were both messy as fuck, but that was on her. They were her friends, not mine!

"Damn! Y'all trying to go to the casino at six o'clock?"

"Uh, excuse you. You know we're going to Golden Nugget in Lake Charles. That's a three-hour trip! You should've been here!"

"Take the kids to your mom's and I'll get them from there once I'm done handling my business," I said.

"It's Valentine's Day Malik!"

"So!"

"My mom has plans too!"

"So, how you know I didn't have plans or does that not matter to you?" I asked.

"I asked you last week if you had plans and you said no!"

"I don't have Valentine's Day plans, but I still have to go check on my dough and shit!"

"And that's more important than your kids?"

"Do you want me to bring them with me? Cuz I can go scoop them up first," I said sarcastically.

"Wow! I can't believe you always do me like this!"

"Do you like what Priscilla? I didn't know you were traveling three hours to go to no fuckin' casino!"

Now I was getting pissed because she was acting like I owed her that shit. My kids weren't supposed to come over to my place until next weekend. Me taking them tonight was me doing a favor for her. She was acting like this was some shit I had to do. Shit, she should've told me that they were going to Lake Charles, but no, she was trying to keep that shit secret from me.

"Never mind! I'll just tell them I'm not going!" she said.

"Well, suit yourself! I was gon' come get them in about an hour!" I said.

"They're already on their way to get me! If I'm not ready when they get here, they're gonna leave me!"

"Then they ain't yo' real friends!"

"No, you aren't my real friend!" she said. She sounded like she was on the verge of tears.

"Who the fuck said we were friends. We're co-parents to our kids, period!" I said.

That was her problem right there. She often mistook my kindness for a weakness and tried to take advantage by calling us friends. We were only "friends" when she needed something. When I needed a favor, she was nowhere to be found.

"Whatever Malik! Happy fucking Valentine's Day!" she said as she ended the call.

The fucking nerve of her! Priscilla's attitude reminded me just of the chick I saw earlier. I was glad I hadn't asked that chick for her number. One like her was enough for me. As I rounded the corner to the trap, I saw a couple of block boys making sales. It made me smile to see that they were on the job. Shit wasn't gonna get done if no one was going to do it. I parked alongside the street and walked up to the front door. I gave the secret knock and the door opened right up.

"S'up Bishop," Keys greeted with a fist bump.

"Nothin' much. What's good?"

"Everything my nigga! Sales is through the roof! Seems like niggas just got paid so everybody looking for something to give them that good feeling. What's good witchu?" Keys asked. "You stopped by before you go get your V Day groove on?"

"Nah, Priscilla looking for me to take the kids tonight," I said.

"Word? Where she finna go?"

"To the casino with her girls is what she said. She just got mad and hung up on me cuz I wasn't there already."

"What? Shit, well, only a gambler will go sit to the casino at six o' fuckin' clock!" he clowned.

"That's the same shit I said, but she claims they going to the casino in Lake Charles."

"Oooooh, okay. Well, shit, you better get going if you finna watch the kids so she can go."

"Shit, she told me never mind. I don't know. I guess I'ma head over there anyway. You got something for me?" I asked.

"Hell yea!" he said. I watched as he walked to the back room and came back with two duffle bags.

He dropped them on the floor at my feet. "Damn!" I marveled. "Now, you know I'ma need help carrying this out right?"

"I already know and I gotchu," he said as he pulled out his AR15. "You already know ain't nobody finna fuck witchu though."

"Yea, I know, but I bet that shit heavy," I said with a chuckle.

"Fuckin' right it's heavy! Wait until you see how much is in these muthafuckas!"

We each grabbed a bag and headed out to my truck. Once we had the bags secured in the floorboard, we shook hands and I hopped behind the wheel. I didn't bother calling Priscilla to let her know that I was on my way because I didn't want to get into it with her ass again. 45 minutes later, I pulled up in front of Priscilla's house. This was a house I purchased for her and our kids after the two of us split up.

We split about six months ago after she caught me cheating... AGAIN!!

I knew that some men cheated without really having a reason. I mean, they had a good woman at home who cooked, cleaned and took care of home. What more did they need to be happy? I cheated because once Priscilla had our second child, it seemed like she no longer gave a shit about herself. Like she just let herself go. She no longer cooked, barely ever cleaned and the sex had gotten boring.

She had put on some weight with our second child, more than the first. She had a hard time getting it to come off. But hell, how the hell did she expect the weight to come off when all she did was sit around all day eating chocolates and snacks. I loved my children more than anything in this world. Riley was five going on 30 and Olivia was two and into everything. We had an agreement that I would get them every other weekend and pay child support on a monthly basis. Sometimes, I gave more than once a month, but it was cool because those were my kids.

I didn't want them to ever go without for any reason. I let myself into the house with my key and the girls came rushing up to me. The music was loud as fuck and the television was on a cartoon for the kids. I didn't know how she expected them to hear anything with the music blasting the way that it was, so I turned the shit down. She came rushing in the living room as soon as I did that.

"Riley didn't I tell... oh, Malik. When did you get here and didn't I tell you to stop using that key to get in?" she fussed. "You gonna make me take my shit from you if you don't start respecting my right to privacy!'"

"Really? You gon' take the key from me on a house I'm still paying for?"

"Well, maybe you should pay it off the way you did your own," she said sarcastically with a crooked smile on her face. "Bottom line, is this my house or yours?" She propped her hand on her puffy hip like she was asking some sort of grand question.

"It's for the girls... everything I do is for my children! You just happen to be enjoying the perks of what I do for them."

"What are you doing here anyway?" Priscilla asked as she smacked her gum. "I told you... never mind!"

"Shit, well, never mind must not mean you ain't going somewhere because clearly you're dressed to go out!" I said.

"So! I ain't gotta report my whereabouts to you no more! We are no longer together, remember?"

"Shit yea, I remember! I just came to get my girls. You can go head on and do whatever you need to," I said. I then turned my attention to my girls. "Do you have your favorite blankie Olivia? Riley what about you? You have your favorite stuffed animal?"

They quickly rushed to their bedroom to get their favorite things to sleep with. They came back a few moments later. "Give your mom a kiss," I said.

"I didn't even pack their bag," Priscilla said.

"No worries. They have clothes at my place."

"Well, excuse me."

"You are."

After the girls were done kissing their mom, I took my five- year old by the hand while I carried her sister and we headed to the truck. I strapped them both in their seats and got in behind the wheel. "Are you girls ready to have fun with daddy?" I asked.

"Yeahhhhh!" They both rejoiced at the same time.

"Do y'all want Happy Meals or Popeye's?" I asked.

"I want a Happy Meal daddy," Riley said.

"You want a Happy Meal? Olivia you want a Happy Meal too?"

She nodded her head, so I drove to McDonald's and got them out of their seats before we headed inside. We stood in line and waited to get to the counter. Then I ordered their Happy Meals and a 10-piece nugget meal for myself. I filled their cups with Sprite while we waited for our food. Once our number was called, I got the tray and led the girls to a table.

"Looks like you got your hands full," a woman said with a smile.

"Yea, but I definitely don't mind one bit," I replied as I returned the smile.

Me and my girls finished our meals then I dumped the tray and headed to the truck. It seemed as soon as we walked outside, there was trouble in the parking lot. A black Dodge Charger came rushing in the parking lot followed by two other vehicles. I stood there for a second curious as to what was going on. Rather than continue to insert my nose into that business, I unlocked the truck and ushered the girls inside. By the time I got them strapped in, it was evident that something was about to go down.

Before I could climb in behind the steering wheel, shots started going off. I hated shit like that, and I blamed myself for sticking around long enough to witness this bullshit. As soon as I saw shit popping off, I should have gotten my girls the fuck out of here. I could hear them screaming inside the truck as I hopped in. I didn't even waste any more time buckling my damn seatbelt because by that time, all hell had broken loose.

This was the type of shit I never wanted my kids to be around. Even though my line of business caused me to draw my weapon from time to time, I never wanted them to be around anything that could put them in danger. What I needed to do was get my kids away from this area as quickly as possible. As shots continued to ring out around me, I heard a couple of bullets hit my truck.

"Aw damn! I'ma fuck somebody up!" I said.

The girls screamed from the back seat as I threw the truck in reverse. "It's okay girls. Daddy is getting y'all away from here right now!" I said.

My tires screeched as I hit the pavement of the highway as I heard sirens approaching. I breathed a sigh of relief because my girls were now safe. If I knew who the fuck had just put my girls in danger like that, I'd look for their asses and fuck them up. That was one thing I didn't take lightly to was someone endangering my precious girls. They meant everything to me.

"You girls alright?" I asked.

"Yea!" Came Riley's shaky voice from the back seat.

I drove to my house anxious to hold my babies in my arms after what they had just been through. Who would've thought a simple trip to McDonald's would have led to what happened next? As I opened the back door, the first thing I noticed was the awkward way that Olivia was slouched forward. I immediately jumped in the back seat and lifted her head to see blood on the front of her shirt. I placed my fingertips against the side of her neck and felt a very weak pulse.

Not trying to scare Riley, I hopped out of the truck and jumped back in the driver's seat.

"Daddy where are we going now?" Riley asked.

"I just have to make a quick trip baby."

"But where?" she asked.

"You'll see," I said.

My heart was racing as I sped in the direction of the hospital at top speed with my blinkers on. I prayed that the police wouldn't pull me over because that was the last thing I needed. I had to get my child to the hospital, and I had to do it fast. The closest hospital was a half hour away, but I made it there in 18 minutes. I pulled up to the emergency room doors and started blasting my horn. Once I got the attention of the staff, I rushed to open the door. That was when I noticed the bullet hole in my truck's rear door.

"My daughter's been shot!" I said in a panicky voice.

The nurse immediately unstrapped Olivia and gently but quickly pulled her from the booster seat. Riley was now whimpering by this time, but I quickly got back in the truck and parked it in a nearby parking spot. I threw the gear shift in park and hopped out to get my Riley from her seat.

"Daddy what happened to Olivia?" she asked in a soft voice.

"She's gonna be okay baby," I replied, praying that I wasn't lying to her.

Tears were threatening to fall from my eyes, but I refused to do that in front of my baby girl. As hard as it was for me to do, I had to keep it together and remain strong for Riley's sake. I rushed into the hospital's emergency entrance and straight to the desk.

"I just dropped my little girl here with a gunshot wound!" I said in a rushed voice.

"Yes, I need to get some information from you please," the woman said.

"I just need to know how my daughter is please!"

"The doctors are working on her. As soon as she's stable, they will come and get you sir. I just need a little information please."

"Yea, sure."

"What's your daughter's name?"

"Olivia, Olivia Rivers!"

"How old is she?"

"She's two."

"What's her birthdate?"

"Uh, June 8th, 2015!" I said.

She asked a few more questions before I remembered I needed to call Priscilla. "I'm sorry. I need to call my baby mama to let her know to come down here," I said. Before she could say anything else, I excused myself. I pulled my phone out and dialed Priscilla's number. She didn't answer the first three calls.

"Gotdammit Priscilla, answer your damn phone!" I said to her voicemail.

"Daddy you cussed," Riley said.

"I know. Daddy's sorry," I said as I hugged her tight as I struggled to hold back my tears.

I sat down with my little girl and prayed like I had never prayed before.

God, I know that I don't come to you often, but I really need you to come through for me. My little girl is so young. I need you to touch on her and cover her in your blood Lord. I need you to help my baby get well. She's only two years old Lord. If you wanna take somebody, please take me. I'd definitely give up my life if you spared my baby's life. So please Lord, take me and let my baby live!

I hit up Keys because I needed to let him know what was going on. I also needed him to look into that incident at McDonald's because somebody had to pay for what happened to my child. "Waddup Bishop?"

"Keys I need you to…" Before I could finish, a doctor walked into the waiting room. "I'ma call you back." I ended the call and walked over to him.

"I'm Dr. Marshall, are you the father of Olivia Rivers?" he asked.

"Yes, yes. How's my daughter?"

"Uhm, do you have someone who could watch your little girl?"

"No, no, I don't. How's Olivia?" I asked.

"Follow me please," he said as I followed him through the double doors. He stopped by an office and stuck his head in. "Alissa would you be so kind as to keep an eye on this little girl while I speak to her father please?"

"Sure Dr. Marshall."

The voice sounded familiar, but I just knew it couldn't be who I thought it was. As soon as she made her appearance, our eyes locked. Hers were solemn and sad, but I could tell that she recognized me too. It was the same chick whose wine bottle busted earlier at the gas station. I had no idea that she worked at this hospital, but then again, how would I know that? It wasn't as if I visited this hospital on the regular. As a matter of fact, up until tonight, I couldn't recall when was the last time I came to this hospital.

"Hey beautiful," she said as she gave her attention to my oldest daughter. "Would you like to come with me to the playroom so your dad can talk to the doctor?"

Riley looked at me as if she was seeking my approval. I nodded with a weak smile to let Riley know it was cool. "It's okay baby. I'll come and get you in a few minutes."

I passed my little girl to the young woman. "Don't worry. I'll take good care of her."

I nodded my head and followed the doctor. As soon as Alissa and Riley disappeared around the corner, Dr.

Marshall turned to me with sad eyes. "This is the part of my job that I hate the most…"

"What are you saying doc?" I asked in a shaky voice.

"I am so sorry…"

"What… what… whaddya mean?" I asked as the tears finally erupted from my eyes. I didn't know why he was apologizing to me.

My daughter had been shot and all I wanted to do was feed her and her sister. I wasn't out there selling no drugs. I wasn't in the street doing nothing I had no business doing. All I was doing was being a father to my daughters.

"We weren't able to save your daughter."

As the reality of his words sunk in, I could feel my breathing intensifying. As I rubbed my hand through my natural curls and rested it on the back of my neck, I felt faint. I leaned against the wall as I stared into the sorrowful eyes of the doctor.

"No! No! That can't be!" I cried. "I brought my daughter to the hospital… to this hospital for you to save her!! Isn't that what you're supposed to do here doctor?! You're supposed to save lives here, right?" I asked. "Right?"

"You're absolutely right. Unfortunately, your little girl's injuries were too severe. We did everything we could to save her, but she was already gone by the time you brought her in."

"No! No! You have to try again! You can't just give up on her!" I said. "You have to try again! She's my baby and she's only two fuckin' years old doc!" I grabbed him by his white coat as tears spilled from my eyes like a river.

"I'm sorry." He wrapped his arms around me as I cried harder than I had ever cried before. When my grandfather died, it was one of the hardest times in my life. I was just a teenager and I thought that was the worse day of my entire life. I was wrong. This was the worst day of my life. After several minutes, the doctor finally asked, "Is there anyone we can call for you?"

I shook my head furiously as the impact of what he just said hit me like a ton of bricks. My little girl was gone. She was dead and she wasn't coming back. I'd never get to hear her laugh or cry again. I'd never get to cuddle with her or rock her to sleep while humming a lullaby to her. I'd never get to watch her grow up and start school, graduate high school or college, get married. She'd never be able to give me any grandchildren. How the fuck did that shit happen?

"The police should be here soon. Because it was a shooting incident, we are required by law to call and report the incident to the police. May I ask what happened?"

"I just took my girls to McDonald's for Happy Meals. That's their favorite place to go. When we were leaving, some cars came speeding into the parking lot. As soon as I heard them arguing, I tried my best to get my children out of there as fast as I could," I said as tears rained from my eyes and down my cheeks.

"So, someone was shooting at you Mr. Rivers?" Dr. Marshall asked.

I was sure he thought it was a drug deal gone bad because of my attire. My pants were sagging, I had diamonds in my ears and a huge diamond cross chain around my neck. Yea, I may have been a thug and sold drugs, but I would have never put my kids in any kind of dangerous situation. That shit at that McDonald's had nothing to do with me or my children. We were just in the wrong place at the wrong time.

"No! Didn't you just hear me say people were arguing, and then they just started shooting. I didn't even realize my little girl had been shot until I got home," I said. "I thought I had gotten them away from there in time! I thought I had saved them!" I was beside myself with grief.

"Wow! I'm so sorry."

"Can I see my daughter?"

"Are you sure?"

"Are you kidding? She's my child. Of course, I'm sure!"

"Okay, follow me," he said as he led the way.

I followed behind him down the long corridor as he walked to an operating room. I took a deep breath as I followed him through the huge white double doors. On the table was my little girl looking smaller than she ever had before. As I slowly approached her, she seemed as if she was sound asleep. I gently picked her up and held her in my arms as I cried while holding her lifeless body. I sunk to the floor and held and rocked my little girl. The sweet scent of her hair invaded my nostrils as I wept over her tiny body.

If it wasn't for the fact that we were inside an operating room, I would've thought this was a bad dream. How could this have happened? How could the three of us have been laughing in McDonald's a little while ago and now my little girl was dead?

"Are you sure I can't call someone for you?" Dr. Marshall asked.

Shit! He couldn't call anyone for me, but I damn sho' could make that call for myself. I still hadn't heard from Priscilla's ratchet ass, and I hadn't called Keys back yet either. Right now though, in this very moment, the only one I needed was the one person I knew could calm me down. I pulled my phone out and called the one person I had always been able to count on since I was a kid.

"Hello."

"Ma..." I cried as I broke down.

"Baby what's wrong? Are you okay? Are the girls okay?"

It was just like my mom to be concerned about me and the girls.

"Ma, I need you to please come meet me..."

"Where are you baby?" she asked.

I could hear her shuffling around as I tried to control my tears long enough to tell her where I was. I wasn't going to tell her what was wrong because I didn't need her panicking on the highway.

"Memorial Hermann ma! The one near the house."

I heard the bell chiming in her car as she cranked the ignition. "Memorial Hermann? What the... never mind baby. I'm on my way!"

I ended the call as someone entered the operating room. She whispered to Dr. Marshall before he approached me.

"Mr. Rivers the police are here to speak to you," Dr. Marshall informed me.

I looked up at that doctor like he had two fucking heads. I knew darn well he saw me with my child. I also

A novel by Lady Lissa

knew that he knew the state that I was in. I wasn't going no fucking where until my mom got here.

Chapter three

Priscilla

When I saw Malik's name pop up on my screen, I intentionally ignored the call. Shit, my girls had decided to wait for me to go to Lake Charles after all, so I wasn't about to let him spoil our good time with his bullshit. He called three more times after, but I continued to ignore him. After the fourth phone call, I turned my phone off. It wasn't that often I got a chance to go out. And it had been a long time since I had been to Louisiana for anything, especially a good time. The last thing I wanted was my baby daddy calling me to rain on my damn parade.

"Damn girl, who keeps blowing up your phone?" Kiki asked as she peered at me around the passenger's seat.

"Ain't nobody but Malik's ass!"

"Aww, yo baby daddy must've wanted some of that for V Day!" Bailey said.

"Girl bye! We ain't doing nothing like that no more!" I scoffed.

"Shit, I don't know why not! Bishop is fine as fuck! If he were my baby daddy, I'd keep fucking him!" Kiki said as she slapped Bailey a high five.

"Oh kay!" Bailey agreed as they laughed.

"Shit, y'all don't know nothing about the real Bishop. If y'all knew him like I did, y'all would feel the same way I do!"

"Bishop got bank! Bishop is fine as hell! And that man is handsome too!" Kiki cooed.

"And he takes care of his kids!" Bailey cosigned.

"Uh huh! If you weren't one of my besties..." Kiki said as she let the rest of her statement fall off.

Shit, she didn't need to finish it because I was tired hearing it. She always said the same thing. If we weren't best friends, she would have made a beeline for my baby daddy a long time ago. I guess she wanted me to consider myself lucky. However, maybe she needed to fuck with him to understand why I wasn't about to put up with his shit no more. But I was glad she had the decency to take our friendship into consideration.

"Can we talk about something else? It's been a while since we hung together."

"Girl we were together two weeks ago!" Bailey commented.

"Yea, but we weren't going to the casino in Lake Charles. Shit, I already ain't got no man, so the last thing I wanna do is think about Bishop all night. I just wanna have fun without thinking about my kids or my baby daddy!" I huffed.

They don't get it. Bishop and I had a good relationship before he started running drugs. Once he started doing that and became the head honcho of our hood, all the bitches started flocking around him like he was Chris Brown. It didn't take him long to start coming home later and later and finally, he stopped coming home for days at a time. I had already given birth to Riley and was pregnant with Olivia when we had that final blow up. There was no way I was going to continue to allow him to disrespect me then come and lay beside me. I thought long and hard before I decided to pack up me and the girls' shit and leave his ass.

At the end of the day, he allowed me to keep the house and purchased another one for himself. The house I had wasn't as big as the one he had, but it was 2800 square feet and the girls and I were comfortable in it. I wasn't sure why he was calling me, but whatever it was would keep until tomorrow. Tonight was all about me and my girls having some fun… no man, no kids, no worries.

It took us four hours to get to the casino because we were in traffic. Once we got there, we headed inside and checked into our room. We went upstairs to drop our bags off to the room and freshen up. About 15 minutes later, we finally made our way to the casino. It was a full house down there and I was ready to enjoy my night. However, I was also hungry.

We had been on the road for what seemed like forever and my stomach was growling. I couldn't wait to eat. "Y'all hungry?" I asked, hoping that Val and Bailey would be just as hungry as I was so I wouldn't have to eat by myself.

"Girl bye! You thinking about food at a time like this?" Kiki asked.

"Hell yea! I'm hungry as hell!" I exclaimed.

"Bailey are you hungry?" Kiki asked her.

"I am, but I can wait to eat. I really would like to get my drink on and play some games. Hell, we're already almost six hours behind!" Bailey responded.

"Well, y'all can go play. I'm going eat," I said as I headed to the buffet table.

The two of them looked at me like I was crazy, but that was on them. As much as I wanted to rush over there and throw some coins in the slot machines, I couldn't do it on an empty stomach. My organs weren't set up that way. So, I made my way to an open table and sat down. I probably looked really lonely sitting there by myself on Valentine's Day, but I didn't care. The server came to my table and introduced herself.

"Will you be dining alone?" she asked.

"Yes. My friends are already inside the casino gambling, but I had to refuel first."

"I totally understand. I'm no good to anyone on an empty stomach," she said with a chuckle.

"Exactly my point."

"Will you be having the buffet or would you like something from the menu?"

"I'll have the buffet."

"What would you like to drink?"

"A strawberry lemonade would be great," I said with a smile.

"Okay. You can just serve yourself and I'll be back with your drink in a couple of minutes," she said as she put a ticket on my table and walked away.

Shit, she didn't have to tell me twice. I jumped up so fast from the table that I bumped into this tall, lanky dude who smelled delicious. I looked up and smiled.

"Excuse me," I said.

"You're excused!" His woman said as she grabbed him by the hand and pulled him away. "Bitch!"

I wanted to snatch that fucking ponytail off her head, but the last thing I needed was to get locked up in Louisiana. I couldn't imagine what Bishop would've said if I had to call him to come bail me out. He would've been pissed. Anyway, I grabbed a couple of plates and made my way around the buffet table filling both plates. To some I might have looked greedy, but if only they knew how hungry I was. All they had to do was spend a little time with me and they would hear my stomach roar like a big bear.

    I finally made my way back to my table and sat down. I dove into my food like Michael Phelps in a pool. I didn't care who was watching me. I was as hungry as a big dog. After devouring both plates of food, I headed to the casino where I hooked up with my girls on the slot machines. Once the drinks started flowing, that was it. The night was LIT!!

    I had so much fun to say that I didn't have a man for Valentine's Day. By the time we got to our room, we were drunk and exhausted. We collapsed in the king-sized bed and I was snoring in minutes.

    The next morning, my girls and I got up around ten o'clock with massive hangovers. However, we had to check out of the hotel by 11, so we didn't have much time to whine about how bad our heads were hurting and spinning. We each took turns hopping in the shower and made it downstairs just in time for check out time. We were 34 miles to Houston before I remembered to turn my phone on. I had totally forgotten about turning it off. I just wanted some time to myself to have some fun.

As soon as I turned my phone on, the notifications started coming in. I had multiple messages from my mom, and she kept asking me to call her, saying it was urgent. What the hell could be so urgent? I was only gone one night. Malik sent me three voicemails, but I decided to call my mom first.

"Damn girl, what's going on with your phone?" Bailey asked.

"All these notifications from my mom and Bishop!" I said with an exasperated breath.

"What's the deal with that?" she asked.

"I don't know. I'm about to call my mom now," I said as I dialed her number.

"Priscilla where the hell have you been? I've been calling you and texting you all night long!" she blasted.

"I went to Lake Charles with Bailey and Kiki. I mean, I ain't got no man, so I thought why not go with them to the casino. We had a blast too!" I said.

"I don't care about your night out! I just wanna know why you weren't answering your damn phone!"

"Mom what's the problem? We're talking now. Did something happen to grandma?" I asked, growing nervous.

"No, nothing happened to your grandmother..." she remarked before I interrupted.

"Thank God! I just don't understand why you're so upset then!"

I could hear her inhale deeply before she spoke. "Nothing happened to your grandmother, but something did happen to one of your babies," she said.

My heart immediately stopped for at least three seconds. What was she talking about? What happened to one of my children? When I left them with their dad last night, they were both fine.

"Mom what are you talking about?" I asked in a shaky tone.

"I don't think I should get into this while you're in the car. Maybe you should come over to my house…"

"No, no, no! You've been trying to reach me all night concerning one of my daughters. What happened to one of my girls?"

"I really think I should tell you this face to face…"

"No mom! You already got me on tens! Tell me now!"

"There was an accident last night…"

"What kind of accident? What happened to my kids, mom?"

"Malik took them to McDonald's on the way home. On the way to the truck, someone started shooting…"

"Oh my God! OH MY GOD!!" I cried as I dropped the phone.

She didn't even have to finish her statement. She said something happened to one of my girls, so that meant one of them got shot.

"What's going on?" Kiki asked as she looked at me.

I couldn't answer as I felt this burning sensation in my chest. As I rubbed my chest to try and soothe the ache nothing seemed to be working. Tears flowed down my cheeks as I tried to keep myself from losing it completely.

"I need you to take me to Bishop's place right away!" I said to Bailey.

"What happened?" she asked.

"I don't know. I just need you to take me there... please!"

"Yea, sure thing," she said. "What's his address?"

I rattled off the address to her and she put it in her navigation system. It took Bailey another half hour to get me to my baby daddy's house.

"Damn! Bishop lives here?" Kiki commented. "This a nice fuckin' house. Damn, you lucky we are friends!"

I didn't even bother to answer her Kiki's ass. At this point, my only concern was finding out what happened to my kids. I just grabbed my purse and my phone off the floor, said a quick thank you to Bailey for driving me and slid out of the car. I rushed to the door like my ass was on fire and started ringing the doorbell and pounding on the door. Finally, after what seemed like forever, Bishop came to the door. He didn't look good at all.

His face was ashen, his eyes were red and puffy, and he looked like he hadn't slept a wink last night. I just barged in and frantically looked around. "Where are the girls?" I asked.

He shut the door and turned to face me with the meanest look that he had ever given me before. "Oh, now you're worried about the girls! Where the hell were you all night Priscilla? I've been calling you constantly and not once did you bother returning one of my fuckin' calls! You even turned your damn phone off, so tell me what was so important that you had to do that huh?"

"Where are the girls Bishop? Please just tell me where they are! Mom said something about some kind of accident," I said as tears spewed from my eyes. "Are they okay?"

"Why didn't you answer your fuckin' phone? Why did you turn the phone off? Did it ever occur to you that I was calling because of an emergency?"

I could tell that Bishop was angry with me, but he needed to push his anger aside and tell me what the hell happened to my children. I was losing my mind standing here and was about to take off running through his big ass house screaming for my children to come running.

"I just wanted to have a little fun okay! What was so important? Where are my kids?!!"

"You should've been here last night! You're their mother, so you should've been here!"

Okay, now he had me scared, especially when I saw tears streaming from his eyes. Bishop never cried or showed any type of emotion like this before. "Please Malik, I know you're upset with me and I'm sorry I wasn't here last night, but I'm here now. Please tell me what happened... please," I begged through trembling lips as the tears fell.

"There was a shooting at the McDonald's last night..."

"Someone was shooting at you?"

"Hell no! I ain't had shit to do with that! I took the girls there to get Happy Meals. When we were done eating, we headed to the truck. Some cars came flying through the parking lot, so I figured some shit was about to start. I tried my best to get the girl strapped and everything before shit popped off. But then they started shooting. I hightailed it out of there as quickly as I could, but..."

"But what Malik?" I asked as my heart raced in my chest.

"But... but when I got home, I noticed that Olivia was scrunched over. When I moved her, I noticed she had blood on her clothes..."

"What... what... what are you saying Malik?" I asked as I shook my head because I already knew what he was gonna say.

"I rushed her to the hospital, but it was too late," he said as he broke down.

"What? My baby's dead?" I asked.

He slowly nodded his head as I opened my mouth and started screaming. This didn't make any sense to me at all. How could my precious little girl be dead? When her dad picked her up last night, she was healthy and happy. How could she be dead now?

"NOOOOO! NOOOO! My baby can't be dead!" I cried as I collapsed against Malik's chest.

He held me as we both cried our eyes out for Olivia. After a few minutes, I became angry though. Something wasn't adding up for me. Why would random people just start shooting at a McDonald's? They had to have been shooting at Malik. With the shit that he did for a living, I knew he had a lot of enemies. This was all his fault.

I pushed myself out of his arms and slapped the shit out of him. "You were supposed to keep them safe! This is your fault with your drug dealing ass..."

I was about to slap him again until Big Mama appeared. "You better put that hand down missy before I use it to drag your ass out of my son's house," she said. She walked up into my personal space and continued her rant. "Now, I know you're upset about Olivia... we all are. But don't you use that as an excuse to make my son feel worse than he already does. This is NOT his fault! He took the girls to McDonald's because they wanted Happy Meals. That shooting that happened was NOT directed at him. You understand me?"

I nodded my head, but I was so heartbroken. All I wanted to do was get my other baby and leave, but shit, I didn't even have a way home. I could kick myself right now.

"It was a stray bullet that struck Olivia. The doctor's tried to save her, but it was too late. She was already gone by the time she was brought in, and that wasn't Malik's fault either. He didn't know she had been struck!" Big Mama continued as Malik cried his eyes out.

"Where is Riley?" I asked.

"She's sleeping. She had an awful night and kept waking up screaming. She just went down for a nap about an hour ago, and so far, she's sleeping good," Big Mama said.

I couldn't imagine how Riley must be feeling. She saw her little sister get shot. I was sure that would give her nightmares. "I need to see her!" I said.

"I think you should wait a while and let her sleep. How about I make us all some coffee, and we can discuss the arrangements we are going to make for our little Olivia?" Big Mama suggested.

I wasn't interested in drinking any coffee. I just wanted to take my daughter home and spend some time with her. I wanted to make sure she was alright. I couldn't believe this shit was happening right now. I had to make funeral arrangements for my baby girl. Once Big Mama left the foyer, Malik led me to the huge living room. His house was way bigger than mine, and nicely decorated for a bachelor. I wondered why a man who lived alone needed such a big house, but I guess with all the money he made, he had to make it big.

I sat down on the plush sectional sofa. Malik sat in the chair opposite me. I could see how broken up he was and maybe I was wrong for blaming him. I just can't believe our daughter was gone. She was only two years old.

"I'm sorry I hit you. I just can't..." The tears began to stream from my eyes again.

Malik rushed over to me and put his arm around me. I leaned against him and cried against his shoulder.

Big Mama came from the kitchen carrying a tray with three cups of coffee, sugar, and cream. She also had three bottles of Dasani water on the tray. I said I didn't want any coffee, but the way my head was spinning right now, I definitely needed it.

"Thank you, Big Mama. Sorry for the way I acted earlier," I said.

"It's okay. I know you're in shock. It's understandable considering what happened. I just want the two of you to come together for the sake of Riley. That little girl doesn't understand everything that went down last night. All she knows is that yesterday she had sister and today, she doesn't. The last thing she needs is to see the two of her parents arguing," Big Mama said.

I had to agree with her on that. For the next couple of hours, the three of us sat together and made funeral arrangements for Olivia. I still couldn't believe this shit was happening. Olivia's body had already been picked up from the funeral home. Tomorrow would be a hard day because Malik and I were going to have to go to the funeral home and pick out a casket for our baby girl. We also had to pick out a dress for her to wear. My heart was in pieces, but we had to push on for the sake of our other daughter, Riley.

God give me strength for what I'm about to go through...

A novel by Lady Lissa

Chapter four

Alissa

Three days later...

    I had looked online yesterday and saw the obituary for the beautiful little girl who was shot a few nights ago. I was shocked to see the same dude that had busted my wine bottle at the hospital that night. He was handsome enough with his boyish good looks, naturally curly hair and beautiful hazel green eyes. He was tall, light brown skin and thuggish. He was so heartbroken for his little girl. I could feel his pain as I looked into his eyes. I wasn't a parent, so I couldn't possibly understand how he felt at that time. To lose a child so young.

    When Dr. Marshall asked me to take the child to the playroom, I had no idea he was talking about that man's child. He didn't even strike me as the type to have children. I don't know why. He just didn't seem like that type.

    Today, he was burying his daughter and I planned to go to the funeral to pay my respects. Not because I knew him, but because I felt sorry for him. I couldn't imagine what he was going through. His mother was just the sweetest person too. She was there for him and his baby girl, lending support and comfort. I was more than sure it didn't take away his pain, but I knew it had to make him feel a little better.

I hadn't seen a baby mama though. I wondered if he was a single dad, and if he wasn't, why the mother hadn't shown up. To me, if the baby's mom was still in the picture, she should've been there. However, I didn't know his situation. I just knew that I was off today, so I was going to go offer my condolences to Malik and his family. As I stood in the mirror checking out my reflection, I smiled at the image that stared back at me. I didn't have many black dresses and didn't feel the need to go out and buy one since I was only going there to show my respects. It wasn't like I was part of the family or anything like that.

I chose to wear the laced long- sleeved bodycon dress. It was just a little above my knees, so I didn't look too sexy. I sprayed on some Gucci Flora Gorgeous Gardenia and slid my petite feet in my black suede laced- up heels. I grabbed my black clutch purse and gave myself one last look in the mirror. Totally happy with what I saw, I smiled my seal of approval before grabbing my keys and phone and heading out the door. I climbed in my dark blue Jeep Grand Cherokee and pulled up the directions to the funeral home on my navigation system. I saw that it would take 45 minutes for me to get there.

The time was now 8:30 and they were supposed to move the body to the church at ten o'clock. I had enough time to make it there if I didn't get stuck in any traffic. On the way to my destination, my mom called.

"Hey mom," I greeted.

"Hey baby, I was calling to see if you wanted to have lunch today."

"Aw, I'd love to mom, but I don't know what time I'll be back home," I answered.

"What do you mean? I thought you were off today."

"I am off, but do you remember me telling you about the little girl that got shot a few nights ago?"

"You mean that poor little baby that was hit by a stray bullet in the McDonald's parking lot?" she asked.

"Yes ma'am."

"Yes, I remember seeing that story on the news and Facebook too. So very sad to lose a child to this senseless violence at such a young age. Why can't these people put these guns down and fight like men? That's how we used to do it in the old days," she said.

"I don't know mom, but you're right, it is very sad. Anyway, I'm on my way to her funeral. I just thought it would be nice if someone from the hospital pay their respects."

"Aw, that's very nice of you baby. I raised such a wonderful daughter."

I always smiled when my mom said that because she was right. I was respectful, ambitious, kind, and smart. I would never do anything that would make my mom disappointed in me. Me and my sister were her pride and joy, especially since our father died when we were young and she had to raise us by herself. I really admired my mom for doing that. She could've fallen apart when our dad died because she was that much in love with him. But she said the reason she didn't was because of me and my sister Shelby. She said that we gave her the strength to push through.

"Yes, you did."

"Well, give me a call back when you get home. Maybe you and Shelby can join me for dinner," she suggested.

"Okay mom, I sure will. Love you," I said.

"Love you too, baby. Talk to you soon."

We ended the call and 25 minutes later, I pulled into the parking lot of the funeral home. It always saddened me when we lost one of our patients. I had been working at the hospital for the past three years. As soon as I got my degree and finished my clinicals, they hired me. I was lucky to have gotten a job so quickly. At 26 years old, I knew exactly where I wanted my career to go.

I had a great job, a beautiful car, and I lived in a lavish condo in the upscale part of town. The only thing missing now was someone to share my life with. Ever since I found out that Maverick had gotten married, I had been in a state of shock. I didn't fester on my problems too long though because of the incident with the little girl getting killed. My grandmother always said that when we thought we had it bad, there was always someone who had it worse. She was right. While I was grieving my dead relationship with Maverick, these people were grieving the death of their precious little girl. It kind of made my problems seem insignificant at the time.

I parked my Jeep and walked into the beautiful funeral home. I signed my name in the guest book before slowly making my way to the front where the casket was. There were a ton of pink and white flowers everywhere, as well as ivy plants and peace lilies. The casket was gorgeous in a blush pink tone with silver trim. I walked up to the casket to see the pretty little girl dressed in a pink frilly dress. I guess pink was her favorite color.

If I didn't know any better, I would've thought she was just sleeping soundly with her favorite blanket tucked by her side. But I knew that wasn't the case. Seeing her lying there caused me to get choked up. I reached in my purse for a tissue as the tears crept along my cheeks. I patted them with the tissue before saying a prayer and walking away.

I turned to see the little girl's family before me. The grandmother I had seen at the hospital sat on the end next to her son. He was holding the little girl I had taken to the playroom. I gathered the woman sitting next to him was the children's mother but couldn't be sure. The whole family looked just as broken up as I imagined they would be. I made my way over to them to offer my condolences.

"I am so sorry for your loss," I said to the grandmother.

She looked up into my eyes and said, "I remember you from the hospital. Thank you so much for coming sweetheart."

"You're welcome."

The little girl immediately recognized me and got excited. "Hi Lissa!" She beamed as she reached up for me to take her. I didn't know if it was appropriate, but her father said it was okay.

I lifted her up and she wrapped her tiny arms around my neck and kissed my cheek. "Can we go to the playroom now?" Riley asked.

"Not now sweetie. You have to stay here with your parents. Maybe another time, okay?"

"Okay."

I returned her to her dad's lap and looked into his red and puffy eyes. "I'm so sorry. I've been praying for you and your family ever since this tragedy happened," I said as he held my hand.

"Thank you. Thank you for coming," he said as he smiled weakly.

"You are welcome."

I could hear the woman whispering to someone else about me, but it didn't matter. Finally, after several minutes of just staring into the father's eyes with my hand still locked in his, he released it. I moved along and offered my condolences to the other family members before taking a seat in the back. After another half hour passed, the funeral home director told people they could view the body once more before it would be taken to the church. I waited as people began filing forward. Then I went behind and said another prayer for this precious little girl who was taken too soon.

As I exited the building, I could hear the screams of the mother, child and father. It really broke my heart to hear the agony this family was going through. It took everything I had to make it to my truck where I broke down and cried. You couldn't help but cry because it was the saddest thing. A little two- year old's life got snuffed out from under her. And for what? Because she wanted was a Happy Meal. Because selfish individuals decided to shoot up a parking lot like they were at the OK Corral.

I waited for the funeral procession to start before I followed behind the cars. I should've gone to the church ahead of everyone else, but it just didn't seem right. To say the funeral service was hard would be putting it mildly. There wasn't a dry eye in the house, especially when the choir started singing *Amazing Grace* and *I Look to You* by Whitney Houston. I decided not to go to the cemetery because to be honest, I was feeling pretty drained by the time the services were over. The last thing I wanted to do was watch them lower this precious child's body in the ground. I just didn't think I'd be able to handle it.

I climbed in my truck and headed home. I just needed a minute to chill before I did anything else. Once I got home, I sat down on the sofa and looked at the beautiful obituary that was printed out of Olivia. There were pictures of her from birth until she passed. I wished Dr. Marshall would've been able to save her that night, but the bullet had entered in her side and traveled. She was pronounced dead on arrival.

My ringing phone drew me from my thoughts. It was Shelby.

"Hey," I answered.

"Hey yourself. How are you feeling? Mom told me you went to that little girl's funeral."

"Yea, I did. I feel really drained. It was just so sad."

"Girl, I can't even imagine. She was a beautiful little girl," she said.

"Yes, she was. You should've seen how she was dressed in the most beautiful pink dress! There were pink and white flowers everywhere!"

"I'll bet. So, not to change the subject, but I will because it's depressing. Are you going to join me and mom for dinner tonight?"

"Uh, yea," I said as I looked at the clock on the wall that said 1:30. "I just need a nap first."

"Perfectly understandable."

"Where are we going?"

"I'm not sure. I think mom wants to go to Razzoo's."

"Well, that's fine with me. I love their crawfish etouffee over dirty rice."

"Me too sis. So, we'll all meet there at seven?"

"Works for me!"

"Cool. See you then."

I ended the call with her and went to change out of my clothes. I slipped into an oversized t-shirt and a pair of boy shorts and headed back to the living room. My alarm clock woke me up at 5:30 that evening and I got dressed to go meet my mom and sister. I always had a great time with the two of them and tonight was no different.

The following week was uneventful until I looked up one day at work and saw Malik. I didn't know what he was doing here, but he had his daughter with him. I was hoping that she wasn't sick or anything. "Lissa! Lissa!" She yelled happily as she reached for me.

I reached out for her and she jumped happily into my arms. "Can we go to the playroom now?" she asked.

How could I refuse her access to the kid's playroom knowing everything she had been through this past week? I wasn't sure why they were here, but if she wanted to play for a little while, I could make that happen. "Sure. Just let me tell the other nurses where I'm going," I said.

I handed her back to her father and walked over to the nurse's station. "Hey girl!" Capri greeted.

"Hey Capri, I have to run down to the second floor for a few minutes. Can you cover for me while I'm gone? I promise not to be too long," I said.

She looked around me at Malik and his daughter. I was more than sure she recognized them from the television or online news reports. She quickly nodded her head. "Take as long as you need. I'll handle things here until you get back," she assured.

"Thanks Capri."

With that, the three of us walked over to the elevators and I hit the 'Down' button. Malik looked different from the last time I saw him. That was good because the last time I saw him, he was crying his eyes out at his baby girl's funeral. The elevator dinged and we hopped on. I hit the button for the second floor, and it whizzed down one flight to the pediatric floor.

When it dinged again, we all stepped off and made our way to the kid's play area. As soon as Riley walked in, she ran to play with another little girl that was in the room. "How is she?" I asked her father.

"She's been having a rough time without her sister. She doesn't quite understand why Olivia isn't here, and I don't really know how to make her understand that she isn't coming back," he said.

"I understand. She's so young."

"Right. That's why I don't want to say the wrong thing," he said. "I'm sorry to just pop up on you at your job like this. I wasn't even sure if you would be here."

"Yep, here I am."

"You've made quite the impression on my little girl. She can't stop talking about you," he said with a smile.

"I imagine I made quite the impression on you as well," I said with a sly smile.

"Yea, you did. I don't think we got off on the right foot, so let me start by apologizing. Clearly, you were having a bad day. I didn't mean to add to your stress. I'm sorry."

"You don't owe me any apologies. You're right, I was having a bad day, but that didn't give me the right to take it out on you. I'm sorry."

"Apology accepted. I'm Malik, Malik Johnson," he said as he reached out his hand.

"Alissa Michaels. Nice to meet you."

"Likewise. So, you're a nurse here huh?"

"Yep. For the past three years."

"Cool."

"What do you do Malik?"

"I'm in sales," he said.

"Really? I've never seen a salesman dressed quite like you," I said.

"I have to be comfortable when I'm working, which I'm not right now."

He was dressed in a Los Angeles Lakers shirt and some jeans, sagging jeans. I didn't want to judge him, but I had a feeling I already knew what he did for a living. I had overheard the doctor and police questioning him that night. They had assumed that he was the target of the shooting that killed his daughter. However, once I listened to his side and watched the news, I realized that we had all been wrong for judging him. That didn't mean I wanted anything more to do with this man than necessary.

If he was into some illegal dealings, I couldn't have that shit nowhere near me. I was a respected woman in the community with a great career path ahead of me. I couldn't allow him to get in the way... no matter how cute his daughter was.

"How have you been since everything?" I was so nervous about asking him that I didn't know how to word my question.

"I'm good. The police have several suspects in custody, so I'm straight. I ain't gonna lie to you. This shit ain't been no walk in the park. My daughter was only two, ya know? I would've gladly traded places with her if that were an option."

"I totally understand. How is your mom?"

"She's doing good. This tragedy has made her want to spend more time with Riley..."

"I can only imagine. The lost of a child or grandchild has a way of bringing people closer together," I said.

A Thug's Romance for Valentine's Day

"Shit, not all people!" he exasperated.

I didn't want to dig into his life that way, but I had a feeling he was speaking on behalf of his baby mama. I had heard her and someone snickering about who I was at the funeral. It shouldn't have mattered who I was as long as I was respectful. The funeral was open to the public, so me coming to pay my respects shouldn't have been an issue.

"Sorry to hear that."

What else could I say? I sensed that he and his baby mama weren't on the best of terms at the funeral. They were sitting next to each other but weren't really speaking. When she cried, she leaned against the woman to her left. He kind of dealt with his grief on his own. Occasionally, his mother put her arm around him but other than that, he was mainly just holding on to his daughter while he grieved for the other one. In that moment and this one, I could tell he loved his kids very much.

"It's cool. No matter what, I'ma always look out for my kids and do right by them."

"I hate to cut this short and I appreciate you for coming by..."

"Yea, I understand you gotta get back to work," he finished.

"Yea, I do."

"Uhm, you got a number where I can reach you? You know, just in case Riley wants to see you again," he explained.

I wasn't sure how I felt about giving him my number. I didn't want him to think that he could call me anytime he felt like it, especially if he was into some illegal dealings. But as I looked over at Riley playing with the other little girl, I realized how hard it was going to be for her without her sister. If I could help her get through it, I would do it. So, I rattled my number off to Malik and stood up.

Riley looked at me and rushed over. "Are you leaving Lissa?"

"Yes honey. I have to get back to work," I said as I stooped to her level.

"Aw, but I don't want you to go," she whined as she wrapped her arms around my neck and held on tightly.

"I know sweetheart, but I have to work. A lot of people come to the hospital so I could help them. But listen, I gave your daddy my phone number, so you can call me anytime you want to."

"For real?" she asked with her head tilted to the side.

"You betcha!" I conceded.

She hugged me again and I hugged her back. She was such a sweet little girl. I wasn't sure how she had attached herself to me so quickly, but she and I had spent a lot of time together the night her sister was killed. An hour and a half had passed before I was paged to bring her back to her father. Maybe that was why.

She finally released me and ran back over to the toys. I stood up and dabbed at my eyes, which had gotten a little misty. "You aight?" Malik asked.

"Yea, I'm fine. Your daughter is really sweet."

"Yea, she is," he said as he looked over at her lovingly.

"Thanks for stopping by," I said.

"Thank you for making the time for us." He reached for my hand and looked me in the eyes as he spoke. There was something about those hazel eyes that caused a flame inside me to erupt.

I quickly pulled my hand away and exited the room. There was no way that I was feeling anything from this man except sympathy for his loss. I had given him my phone number, but it wasn't so we could get involved. I had just broken up with Maverick's low- down dirty dog ass. No way was I about to get involved with another man who could possibly be just like him.

I headed to the elevator and quickly pressed the button to go back upstairs. However, physically getting away from that man was easier than mentally. Thoughts of Malik and his daughter plagued my mind the rest of

A novel by Lady Lissa

the afternoon. I didn't know what was wrong with me, but something was stirring up in me.

"I will not get involved with that man!"

Chapter five

Malik

This past week had been a really rough one. My little girl kept looking for her sister who of course wasn't there. I tried explaining to her that her sister was in heaven, but she was too young to understand. I eventually told her that Olivia was an angel that got loaned to us from God, and that she had to go home because he needed her back. That started another conversation that I wasn't ready for.

"Am I an angel too daddy?" Riley asked.

"Yes baby, you are."

"So, how come God didn't want me?"

"Because daddy needed you to stay with him. If both of you went home to God, who would daddy have left?" I asked.

She wrapped her little arms around my neck and said, "It's okay daddy. I'll stay with you." Then she looked up at the ceiling and said, "You can't take me yet Mr. God. My daddy needs me to keep him company."

A single tear slipped from my eye, but I quickly brushed it away before she saw it. "Daddy can we go see my friend?"

"Who's your friend baby?"

"Lissa! I wanna go play at the playroom," she said excitedly.

"Oh, well, daddy doesn't know how to reach her. I don't know if she's working," I said.

"Can we go see her?"

"Well, you have early dismissal on Friday, so maybe we can go then."

"Yaay!" she said happily.

"Let's go get you ready for bed. You have school tomorrow."

We headed to her bedroom so I could tuck her in. "Daddy can you read me a story?"

"Sure can. What would you like me to read?" I asked as she climbed in bed.

"The Animals Kiss Good Night."

I knew exactly which book she was talking about even though she didn't say the title exactly right. I looked in her little pink bookcase and grabbed the book, *If Animals Kissed Good Night*. I sat on the side of her bed, opened the book, and began to read. By the time I got to the end, she was softly snoring. I stood up and kissed her forehead while pulling the cover under her chin. I placed the book back on the shelf and glanced over at the empty bed that used to be Olivia's.

What I wouldn't give to see her cute little face again. What I wouldn't give to feel her tiny lips kiss my cheek. What I missed most was her telling me that she loved me. Before I could get too emotional, I walked out of the room. I decided that the next day, I would take Riley to see the nurse at the hospital. Hopefully, she could help to lift my little girl's spirits, especially since she had been asking for her since the funeral.

The following day, I told Riley I had a surprise for her. I strapped her in her seat, and we made our way to the hospital. Once there, I really wasn't sure where to go, so I had to ask the receptionist. She told me that Alissa was working on the fourth floor, so me and Riley headed to the elevators and pressed the 'Up' button. Once the elevator opened, we hopped in the car and I hit the number four button on the panel. As the elevator came to a halt on the fourth floor, we headed to the nurse's station. Before I had a chance to ask for Alissa, we spotted her down the corridor. Thank God because I had no idea what her last name was.

Riley immediately perked up and I could tell that Alissa was equally happy to see her. As she and I chatted in the kid's area while Riley played, she didn't seem anything like the person I met on Valentine's Day last week. She seemed more put together and content. Hell, that was a horrible day for both of us, so I'm sure I seemed like a different man to her also.

When she gave me her number for Riley, I knew that I'd be using it for myself. Shit, why not? She was a beautiful woman and even though we got off to a rocky start, the chemistry between us was there. I could tell from the way she acted when I touched her. She didn't have to jump sky high for me to know that we had sparks. Hell, the whole time she was sitting next to me, I had to mentally fight with my dick to stay in check. That nigga had been fighting to say hello since the jump.

After we said our goodbyes, I allowed Riley to play for a few more minutes. Now that her little sister was gone, she didn't have anyone to play with but me and her mom. And let's not talk about Priscilla because ever since the funeral, that bitch had been on some other shit. I was surprised she had let me take Riley on Thursday considering it wasn't even my weekend. I checked the time on my watch and saw that it was almost three in the afternoon. Riley and I headed towards the elevators and I hit the 'Down' button.

"Daddy can we go see Big Mama?" Riley asked.

"You wanna go see Big Mama?" I asked as I looked down at her.

So, that was where we went... to my mom's house.

When we got there, Riley jumped into my mom's arms. The two of them were very happy to see each other. "Daddy can I spend the night with Big Mama?" Riley asked a half hour later.

"That's up to Big Mama, baby."

"Big Mama can I stay the night with you?"

"Sure baby! I would love that," my mom said.

So, with the two of them all happy and content, I left the house. I decided to head over to the trap house to check on things since I was free for the evening. However, I couldn't get Alissa off of my mind. There was something about that young woman that had me intrigued to say the least. I just wanted to get to know more about her. I guess it had a lot to do with her compassion for my child and me. She even showed up at the funeral services for Olivia. That meant a lot to me even though I didn't let her know at the time.

On the way to the trap, I decided to give her a call. I knew she gave me her number for Riley to contact her, so I hoped she wouldn't get angry with me for using the number for myself.

"This is Alissa," she answered.

"Hi Alissa, it's Malik."

"Malik? Is everything alright with Riley?"

"Everything is fine with her. She's actually visiting with my mom for the evening..."

"Oh, okay. So, what can I do for you Malik?"

"Well, since I had a free evening, I was just wondering if I could see you later. You know, when you get off work..."

"Uhhhh, I don't know..." she said. "I mean, why do you want to see me?"

"Can I be honest with you?"

"No, I'd like you to lie to me and not stop," she said sarcastically.

I chuckled at her humor even though I knew she was being sarcastic. "Okay, I asked for that."

"Yea, you did."

"Look Alissa, the truth of the matter is that I haven't been able to stop thinking about you. Ever since the night we met, you have been on my mind. I just thought..."

"Thought what? That you would use your daughter to take advantage of me?"

"Hell no! And if you think after what happened to my youngest daughter that I'd do something like that to my oldest daughter, then you really don't need to know a nigga like me!"

That shit had pissed me off. She didn't know a damn thing about me, but she was insinuating some bullshit that couldn't be further from the truth. The only reason I had taken Riley to see her ass was because she wanted to go. Of course, I wanted to see her also, but I didn't go there for me. I went there for my daughter.

"Sorry. I guess that was the wrong thing to say. I see how much you love your daughter, so I shouldn't have said that."

"No, you shouldn't have. After everything that happened with Olivia, I would never use Riley in any kind of way. The reason we went to the hospital to see you earlier was because she wanted to see you! She specifically asked me to take her to visit you! That was NOT my idea!"

"I get it, and I apologize again."

"Apology accepted. Maybe this was a bad idea. Sorry I bothered you," I said.

Before she could say anything else, I ended the call. I didn't have time for this shit. I didn't know what the fuck she thought this was, but I definitely wasn't going to be chasing after a chick who thought I had to use my child to get her fucking attention.

For the next six months, I busied myself with business and my daughter. Nothing could ever get me to forget about my youngest daughter, but I took great pride knowing that the dude who was responsible was no longer breathing. He was arrested a week after my daughter was buried. A warrant had been issued for his arrest, but they couldn't find his ass. If it wouldn't have been for the price I put on his head, he most likely would have disappeared off the grid.

Once he was locked up, I got word to a couple of my men on the inside that I needed that situation handled. Before that nigga had the chance to enter a plea, I had his life snuffed out. That nigga had a lot of nerve walking around here breathing after taking my baby girl's life.

Now that his ass was out of the picture, I could breathe a bit easier. I hadn't seen Alissa once in the past six months, even though Riley had asked for her a few times over the first month. Eventually, she stopped asking me though. I was happy about that. Her mom and I had gotten into several major blow ups about Alissa because Riley had mentioned her. I didn't understand why my baby mama thought it was any of her business what was going on in my life. I mean, she was out there partying every fucking weekend from Thursday to Sunday with no complaints from me.

As long as she didn't bring some strange nigga around my daughter, I was cool with whatever else she was doing. I had just gotten home after being in the streets all day, so I was pretty exhausted. All I wanted to do was hop in the shower, heat up some Ramen noodles and go to sleep. I had just gotten out the shower when I heard my doorbell ringing. Who the fuck was at my door at this time of night?

I wrapped a towel around my waist and went to the door. I peeked through the peephole and was surprised by who was on my doorstep. What the fuck was she doing here? The only way I was going to get an answer to that question was to open the door, so I turned off the security alarm and unlocked the door. I pulled it back to find Kiki standing there with a coat on. It wasn't even cold outside, so my guard immediately went up.

"What the hell are you doing here Kiki?"

She walked by me as if I had invited her ass in. "I came to see you."

"About what?" I closed the door and stood there with my arms across my chest.

"About us."

Now this girl was tripping. What the hell was she talking about? There was no us!

"Us? Girl stop trippin'!" I said.

"I'm not tripping. You know I've always had a thing for you. And with the way you're dressed right now, looks like you were expecting me," she said as she approached me.

I held my hand up and said, "Whoa nah! I don't know what the fuck you think this is, but…"

I couldn't even finish my sentence because she dropped her coat and revealed her naked body. Now, I would've refused to fuck her ass because she was my baby mama's bestie, but at the end of the day, I was a man. My dick immediately thrust outward as she smiled.

She quickly closed the gap between us and removed my towel. Then she dropped to her knees and started sucking my dick like a lollipop. I was surprised by what she was doing, but if she wanted to suck my dick, I was going to let her.

"Mmmm!" She moaned as she licked around the head and thrust it back in her mouth.

Kiki was fine as fuck, but I never would've crossed that line with her since she and my baby mama were close. But damn! If she didn't tell, I sure wouldn't. After several minutes, I reached into the small table in the foyer and pulled out a condom. Shit, I had condoms all around the house because I never knew where or when I'd get the urge to fuck.

I strapped up and threw her over the back of the sofa and banged her out from behind. After a good 20 minutes, I released into the latex protector. I pulled out and she practically fell to the floor. I grabbed her and tried to steady her on her feet.

"You good?" I asked.

"Yea. Somehow, I imaged this going differently," she said.

"Differently how?" I asked as I walked over and grabbed the towel off the floor.

I grabbed a Kleenex from the box on the coffee table and removed the used condom from my dick. I made my way to the half bath and flushed the contents. I wrapped the towel around my waist and made my way back to the living room.

"I just imagined spending the night."

"Why would you think that?" I asked with a confused look on my face. "I mean, I ain't invite you over here."

"You didn't tell me to go either."

"How could I once you dropped that coat and showed yo ass?"

"So now what?"

"What do you mean now what?" I asked.

"We just had sex, so what are we now?"

I didn't know what the hell she was asking me. "We're done, that's what we are!" I said with a laugh.

"Really Bishop? You just gon' use me like this and then say we're done?"

"I didn't use you! If anything, you practically threw that pussy at me!"

"Wow! I see you!" she said.

"Shit, I'm glad you do."

"I guess I'll have to let Priscilla know about this," she threatened.

I couldn't laugh any harder if she had told a Kevin Hart joke.

"Tell Priscilla? You think I give a fuck if you tell my baby mama we fucked?"

"I'm sure that's some information you wanna keep from her."

"You out yo fuckin' mind! I don't give a shit who you tell! Now, if you will excuse me, I'm finna jump back in the shower before I hop in bed."

I began walking towards the front door as she stood there looking surprised.

"You really gon' just throw me out?" She had the nerve to ask. "After we just had sex!"

"After we fucked! That's what we did... we fucked!" I corrected. "What the fuck you thought was gonna come from that shit?"

"I don't know! But I certainly didn't think you were gonna throw me out as soon as we were done!"

"Then you don't know me as well as you thought you did huh?" I retorted. I pulled the door open and ushered her out of it.

"I thought you were better than this Bishop!"

"Oh, you ain't heard?"

"Heard what?" she asked as she walked out the door.

"I'm a savage!"

With that being said, I shut the door and locked it. I watched her on the Ring doorbell to see what her next move was going to be. When I saw her lift her foot to kick my door, I said, "Do it! I wanna see you do it, so I'll have a reason to whoop yo ass!"

She huffed and turned on her heels. Just as I thought she would. Shit, she knew better! I wasn't a woman beater or anything like that, but I would've slid her one had she fucked up my damn door.

Chapter six

Kiki

Well, I certainly hadn't expected shit to turn out like that when I decided to pop up on Bishop. I had been wanting him for a while, but tonight the urge was strong. I figured if I showed up with nothing under my coat, he'd take the hint. Well, he took the hint, but not the way I wanted him to. How come he didn't take me to the bedroom? How come he didn't let me stay the night? That nigga fucked me while he had me bent over the back of the sofa, which was uncomfortable as hell. I just thought he couldn't wait to get some which was why he took it that way. I damn sure didn't think he was going to throw me out of his house after he got what he wanted.

That nigga pissed me all the way off with that shit. Then he had the nerve to watch me on his fucking doorbell camera. Good thing too because I would've left a dent in that fucking door. I stomped off to my car madder than a pit bull having to share his food with another dog. I got in and burned rubber out of his driveway.

"Got that big ass house and don't wanna share it with a bitch! What the fuck he keeping that big fuckin' house to himself for?!" I fumed to myself.

I wanted to call Priscilla but knew she would blow a gasket. I called Bailey to see what she was going to advise me to do. What I hoped she wasn't going to do was tell me something that would piss me off more than I was already.

"Hey girl," she answered.

"Girl, I am so pissed!"

"Girl, you always got some drama in your life when we aren't around. What happened now?" Bailey asked.

"So, don't judge me alright? I'm feeling bad enough already," I said.

"What are you talking about?"

"So, I finally got up the nerve to go to Bishop's house..."

"Wait! You did what?" Bailey asked.

"I went to Bishop's house!"

"Why?"

"Because I'm tired lusting over him. I wanted to see..."

"No, no, no! Please don't tell me what I think you're gonna tell me."

"What?"

"That you fucked Bishop!"

"How did you know that?"

"Oh my God! Why would you do that? You and Priscilla are best friends!"

"No, you and Priscilla are best friends," I corrected. "I don't really like her ass like that!"

"Wooooow! Are you serious right now?"

"Damn right!"

"How could you not like her and I didn't even know?" Bailey asked.

"Because I'm a great actress," I said with a smile.

"Well, damn bitch! Do you feel that way about me too?"

"Girl bye! You and I have been friends for way too long for me to feel that way about you! Stop playin'!"

"I'm not playing, but you're obviously very good at lying," she said.

"I guess you could say that. Anyway, I didn't call to talk about Priscilla! I called to tell you about me and Bishop!" I said. "Do you know that nigga let me go down on him, strapped up then threw me over the back of the sofa and fucked me like I wasn't shit?"

"What?" I could hear in her voice that she was finding this shit humorous, but I didn't think it was funny at all.

"It's not funny Bailey!" I said with an attitude.

"I'm sorry. I don't mean to laugh, but what did you expect? The two of you aren't in any kind of relationship," she said.

"I know that. I was just hoping…"

"Hoping that he would be your man? Are you out of your mind?!"

"No! I'm not! What I really wanted was to get pregnant by him and give him another kid! But of course, he strapped up so ain't no way I'm pregnant!"

"Bish, no you were not trying to get pregnant by Priscilla's baby daddy!"

"Yes, I was! I would've been set for life just like that bitch!"

"Well, I'm glad he strapped up! The last thing I'd want is to be put in the middle of the drama between you two!" Bailey said.

"Man, I'm so mad!"

"Don't be! That was just the work of God! You do not belong with Bishop, so you certainly don't need to be having a baby by him!"

"Let you tell it! I knew you weren't going to be supportive of me. You're always so supportive of Priscilla, but when it comes to me…"

"Don't do that! Don't you dare do that!" she said angrily. "I'm just as supportive of you as I am of

Priscilla... when you make sound decisions. This right here is not a sound decision!"

"That's your opinion!" I said. "I'm about to go home and soak in the tub. Even though we fucked in the most uncomfortable position, that nigga still tore this pussy up!"

"TMI bitch, TMI!"

"Talk to you tomorrow," I said.

"Good night," Bailey said and hung the phone up.

My plan backfired because I wanted to spend the night with Bishop. I wanted to wake him for sex in the middle of the night and pop up pregnant. I wanted to take pictures of the two of us in bed together and show Priscilla that she ain't the only one who could fuck a baller! But that nigga wanted no parts of the shit!

"Ugh! Now what am I gonna do?" I asked myself out loud while blowing an exasperated breath. "I'll think of something."

I pulled into the parking lot of my apartment complex and parked in front of my door. I rolled my eyes when I saw Jason's truck parked there. "What the hell does he want?"

I slid out of my car as he climbed out of his truck. "Where the fuck you been Kiki?"

"None of your damn business Jason! We aren't together anymore!" I fussed. "What the hell are you doing here anyway?"

"Don't fuckin' talk to me like that!"

"I talk to you how I want to! You're over here invading my damn space... UNIVITED!"

"I don't give a fuck if I'm uninvited! Where the fuck were you?"

"About my business!" I said as I twisted my neck and shit.

"You still carrying my baby! So, no matter what the fuck you think, as long as you're carrying my kid, your whereabouts are my fucking business!"

Shit! I forgot he knew that I was pregnant. He and I hadn't spoken since I told him I was pregnant, so I assumed he wasn't ready to be a dad. When we broke up, I happily took my ass to the women's clinic and terminated that pregnancy. There was no more damn baby! That was why I wanted a kid for Bishop. Having a baby by Bishop would set me up for the rest of my life. I'd most likely be on Section 8 and food stamps if I had a baby by Jason.

However, now was definitely not the time to tell this fool about the abortion.

"My business is my business just like yours is your business! Why weren't you checking for me when you had your dick stuffed between Theresa's old nasty ass? Huh?"

"Man, I told you that bitch didn't mean shit to me! She threw the pussy at me and like any nigga, I took it I shouldn't have since we were together, but I did what any other nigga would've done if he was in that situation!"

Niggas so damn stupid! That was the same thing that Bishop had just said.

"You know what? I don't even care anymore! Just get yo ass away from here!" I said.

"I'm not leaving until you tell me where the fuck you were! And what the fuck you doing with a coat on in the hottest month of the fuckin' summer?!" Jason fumed.

"That's also none of your business!"

"Kiki I'm not playin' with you girl! You better tell me where the fuck you was!"

"Boy bye! I don't owe you shit! We ain't together no more," I retorted. "Now, you got two minutes to get away from my house before I call the police on your ass for trespassing!"

"Bitch you got me fucked up!"

"Bitch?! Oh, now I'm a bitch!"

"You been a bitch!" Jason continued.

I didn't even bother to answer him as I pulled out my phone and headed inside my apartment. I shut the door before he could try and block me from closing it. The nerve of that asshole. Shit, I thought he was going to open my damn coat right there in the parking lot. Would've been pussy juices everywhere since I had nothing on underneath. I hurriedly made my way to the bathroom so I could take a shower.

"Why couldn't my plan have worked?" I whined as I turned on the water.

Shit, I ain't giving up though...

Chapter seven

Malik aka Bishop

Sleeping with Kiki was a disaster that should've never happened. I regretted fucking her as soon as I busted that nut, but what could I do about it now? It was too late to stop and there was no way to rewind the hands of the clock. All I could do was throw her skanky ass out and take another shower. I wished Priscilla had never shown those bitches where the fuck I lived. Not many people knew where I rested my head and I wanted to keep it that way. Now that Kiki knew, ain't no telling who else she would tell. I should've shut the door in her face when I realized it was her. Hell, I shouldn't have opened the door. Coulda, woulda, shoulda... it didn't even matter now.

A week had passed and thankfully, she had stayed the hell out of my way. I guess she hadn't told Priscilla about that night because she never mentioned it. Two months after me and her slept together that bitch had the nerve to pop up with a positive pregnancy test. I almost died laughing at her ass. I didn't give two fucks if she was pregnant because I knew that wasn't my kid.

I made damn sure to protect myself. She would never catch me slipping.

"Like it or not, we are having a baby!" Kiki fussed.

"Girl bye! I didn't even nut in yo ol' crusty ass, so miss me with the bullshit!"

"Why is it so hard for you to believe that you knocked me up Bishop? I thought you would at least be a little excited! I mean, you lost a baby and now I'm gonna give you another one!" she said with a lopsided grin.

That shit sent me from zero to a hundred real quick. I rushed up in her face and pointed my forefinger all up in her grill. "Bitch don't you ever mention my daughter again! I don't know who lil mutt you carrying but it ain't mine!" I fumed. "Now, if you know what the fuck is good for you, you best not ever bring yo ol' dry ass around my house again!"

"Dry ass? Crusty ass? It wasn't dry and crusty when we was fucking though!"

"Shit, yes it was! I don't know who lied to you, but that pussy was dry dry! That's why I kept spitting on it otherwise, my dick would've been full of carpet burns from that muthafucka!"

"Fuck you Bishop! FUCK YOU!"

This bitch was lucky I wasn't the same nigga I was before my daughter died. She wouldn't have got the first fuck you out of her mouth let alone a second one.

"For the sake of my daughter, I'ma let you walk away from here with yo teeth still attached to those black gums in yo mouth. Just know that if it wasn't for her, I would've knocked you clean into the middle of next month. NOW GET YO FUCKIN' ASS OFF MY PROPERTY BEFORE I SHOOT YOU AND GET RID OF YO DAMN BODY!!" I threatened.

Shit, she took off like fire was in her draws after that. She knew the type of nigga I was and also knew I didn't make idle threats. She backed out of my driveway so fucking fast, she left a hubcap behind. I just shook my head as I picked the damn thing up and tossed it in the Waste Management garbage can. I hadn't heard from her since.

I had to run to Walmart to pick up some things for my weekend with my baby girl. I had to pick her up from school this afternoon and she wanted to watch a movie with popcorn. So, of course, I needed the popcorn.

As I was walking towards the entrance of the Walmart, a figure caught my eye. It couldn't be her. That was the first thought that ran through my head. But it had to be her. She was the only one who was that short with a body like that. As I practically jogged the rest of the way to find her, I entered the store. Searching quickly to my left and right, I didn't see her at all.

"Damn! Where the hell did she go?" I asked myself.

Walmart Supercenter is a big ass store, so finding out which way she went would be like a needle in a haystack. What I did was grabbed a small cart and went to get the things I needed. I couldn't afford to waste any time because I had to pick my daughter up from school at 3:40 and it was already 1:30. I headed back up front to check out praying that I would see her before I left.

Luck was definitely on my side because as soon as I made it to the front, I saw her heading for the register. I swear if they would've had a speed limit as to how fast these carts could be pushed in Walmart, I would've gotten a ticket. I got right behind her and tapped her on the shoulder. She turned around with a surprised expression on her face.

"Malik?" she asked.

"Yep," I said with a smile as I reached out to hug her.

Damn! She smelled so good and her body felt like it had melted against mine. I didn't know how long we had been standing there like that, but the cashier cleared her throat, so we separated. She glanced at me shyly as she pushed her cart to the register and started loading her items.

"How've you been? How's your mom and Riley doing?" Alissa asked.

"I've been good. Big Mama is fine, and Riley is doing great! She celebrated her sixth birthday a couple of months ago," I informed her.

"Wow! She must be growing."

"Like a weed," I laughed. "You look great! It's been a long time."

"Thank you. I know it has. You look good too," she said with a smile.

The cashier gave her the total and she slid her debit card into the machine. The cashier handed her the receipt and she thanked her.

I had already loaded my items on the belt, so the cashier turned her attention to me. She greeted me with a smile as big as a kid who just sat on Santa's lap. Alissa stood there waiting for me and I was happy about that. I hadn't realized how much I wanted her until just now. Even though I had her phone number, I hadn't used it after our last conversation because it had rubbed me the wrong way. But I was willing to put all that behind us now. Shit, it was in the past anyway and she had apologized.

I paid for my items and the two of us walked out together. "So, you're off today?" I asked.

"I'm actually off for the weekend," she said.

"Cool. Any big plans for your weekend?"

"Not really. I just planned to get some rest."

"Oh okay. Well, how about you come over to my place later?" I boldly asked.

"Your place? Is this your way of asking me out?" Alissa asked as she glanced at me sideways.

"Yes and no."

"What does that mean?"

"I'm asking you out, but it's my weekend to spend with my daughter. She asked to watch a movie with popcorn, so I'd like it if you could join us. I'm sure Riley would love to see you," I added.

Once we got to her car, I helped her put her bags inside before she turned to me and we continued our conversation.

"I would love to see her too. You think she remembers me?" Alissa asked.

"I bet she does."

"Do you still have my number?"

"If it hasn't changed."

"It hasn't," she smiled.

"Then I got it."

"Text me your address then. What time do you want me to come?"

"Seven or 6:30, either one."

"Okay. It was good seeing you Malik," she said.

"Don't say it like you won't be seeing me later," I coaxed.

"That's not what I'm saying at all." Her beautiful smile could light up any room. She definitely had my heart beating super fast. I wasn't sure why we had lost contact before, but I'd make sure we didn't lose it again.

"Good, because I'm looking forward to spending time with you. Can I get another hug?" I asked.

"Sure," she said.

I opened my arms and wrapped them around her. As I held her close, I leaned forward and inhaled the fresh scent of her hair. It smelled like flowers and honey or some shit like that.

A couple of minutes later, a lady walked by and made a comment about the two of us getting a room. Alissa and I chuckled as she reluctantly pushed herself out of my arms. "See you later," she said.

I opened the door to her car, and she slid in behind the wheel. "I can't wait!" I said.

She started her car and with a wave of her hand, she backed out of the parking spot and left. I finally snapped out of my trance and walked over to my truck. I placed my bags in the back and hopped in the driver's seat. I smiled as I thought about how fate made it possible for me and Alissa to see each other again. I couldn't wait until she and Riley saw each other tonight. My little girl was going to be so excited and happy.

Since the death of Olivia, things hadn't been very easy for Riley. She kept wondering why her sister hadn't come home yet. She wondered where she was. I had tried explaining things to her and thought she understood, but she didn't get it until months later. She finally grasped the fact that her little sister was gone and not coming back. I decided to remove Olivia's bed out of the room that they shared at my house. I did that to help Riley cope better with her sister's loss.

I checked the time on the dashboard and saw that it was almost 3:15. I might as well head to the school to wait for Riley to get out. I pulled up to the school at exactly 3:50 and I was glad because mostly all the cars were gone from the pickup line. I pulled in behind a black Nissan Altima and waited for the line to move. Once it was my turn, I pulled up and picked up my baby girl. I stopped by McDonald's, not the same one where Olivia got shot at, and got her a Happy Meal from the drive-thru.

Then we headed home. She rattled the whole way home about how her day was at school. Once we got home, I sat her at her little table for her to eat. When she was done, I gave her a bath. "Why am I taking a bath so early daddy?" Riley asked.

"Well, I have a surprise for you. And we're watching movies tonight, so you needed to get cleaned up before we started watching. Just in case you decide to fall asleep," I said.

"What's my surprise daddy?"

"You'll find out soon enough," I said with a huge smile.

It was almost five o'clock, and I was starting to get anxious to see Alissa.

"Do you have homework today?"

"Not on Fridays daddy!"

"Oh yea! I forgot today was Friday. Well, do you color for a little while?" I asked.

"Yeaaaaa!" So, for the next hour and a half, the two of us colored and chatted.

When the doorbell rang at 6:40, I got up to go answer it. Riley followed behind me curious to find out who was at the door. As I swung the door open, Alissa smiled at me.

"Glad you could make it," I said sincerely.

"Thanks for inviting me," she responded as she looked at Riley.

She got down on her knees and looked at my little girl. She didn't even need to do that considering they were almost the same damn height. "Hey Riley! Do you remember me?" Alissa asked.

She nodded her head slowly but didn't say anything.

"Are you sure?" Alissa asked.

"Lissa from the hospital," Riley said in her little small voice.

Next thing I knew, she had fell into Alissa's arms and was hugging her tightly. The look on Alissa's face as she hugged my little girl was one of pure joy. I had no idea the bond they shared had gone to this extent.

After they finished their greeting, I leaned in to give Alissa a hug. She looked good as fuck in those short shorts and a black t-shirt. "I thought I had pulled into the wrong driveway," she said as she looked around.

"Why you say that?" I asked.

"Look at this place! It's huge!"

"It's not that big," I smiled.

"It's way bigger than any house I've ever been in."

"Well, let us show you around," I said as Riley grabbed her hand.

The two of them followed me through the house. The house consisted of four bedrooms and three and a half bathrooms. There was a huge kitchen with cherry wood cabinets and stainless- steel appliances. I had a living room, formal dining room, family room and the backyard was huge. I had a big swing set for the girls but ever since Olivia's death, I had trouble getting Riley to swing on it.

Once the tour was done, Alissa blew out an exasperated breath. "Whew! Yea, this house is huge!"

"It's not that big," I said again with a laugh.

"Uh huh," she said as she looked at me.

The three of us sat on the sofa and I grabbed the remote to the 65- inch television that was mounted on the wall. "So, what should we watch?" I asked as I turned the TV on.

"FROZEN 2!!" Riley yelled excitedly.

I pressed the blue microphone in the center of my remote control. "Frozen 2!" I spoke clearly. The channel changed to the Disney movie Frozen 2. "Alissa have you eaten? I can order pizza."

"Yaaaay!" Riley shouted excitedly.

"That's fine," Alissa responded.

So, I logged on to the Pizza Hut app and ordered pizza, wings and cheesy bread. I put the movie on and the three of us watched it until the doorbell ran 45 minutes later. I got up to go get the food and pay the driver. Then I headed back to the living room and put the boxes on the coffee table. I made my way to the kitchen to grab three plates.

"Alissa!" I called out. She and Riley came to the kitchen. "What would you like to drink?"

A Thug's Romance for Valentine's Day

"What do you have?"

"Anything you want… even that Sutter Home's wine from that last time," I clowned.

She smirked at me sideways. "You got jokes, huh?"

"I suppose, but I really do have that wine. Would you like a glass?"

"Sure, if it won't be a problem to drink it in front of Riley."

"It's cool. She can have some Kool-Aid," I said.

"I love strawberry Kool-Aid!" Riley chimed in.

I poured Riley a cup of Kool-Aid and Alissa a glass of wine and grabbed a cold Heineken beer for myself. We headed back to the living room to eat and finish the movie. By the time we were done eating and the movie was over, Riley was knocked out against Alissa's boob. Alissa had draped an arm around her a while ago as she softly purred.

"I'm gonna go tuck her in," I said as I lifted my little girl off the sofa.

"Okay. I'll clean this up," Alissa said as she stood up.

"I can get that when I get back."

"It's okay. I don't mind."

I left the room to put my baby to bed. She was really tired because she didn't even peek or say anything when I put her down. I tucked her cover and kissed her cheek.

As I made my way back down the hallway, I could hear Alissa still in the kitchen. She had put the dishes in the dishwasher and seemed to be waiting for me.

"You think I could have another glass of wine?"

"Sure."

I reached in the refrigerator and grabbed the bottle I poured her another glass and poured some Remy for myself. I replaced the bottles in the fridge, and we made our way back to the living room.

"Are you having fun?" I asked.

"I am. I'm enjoying myself very much," she said.

The two of us sat on the sofa and relaxed as the television played. I didn't know if it was the alcohol or what, but her thighs were looking real good. I traced my fingertip along her thigh as she stared at me intently.

"I wanna kiss you so bad right now," I said in a husky voice.

"Are you waiting for permission?"

"Well, I know you got that lil feisty attitude and shit. I ain't trying to get my ass smacked the fuck out!" I laughed and she joined in.

"You can rest assured that if you kiss me, I won't smack you."

That was all I needed to press my lips against hers. She moaned deeply as I thrust my tongue deep in her sweet mouth. I wasn't sure what was going to come from this kiss, but the heat building up inside me made me want to take it all the way. All she had to do was give me the green light and it was on.

A novel by Lady Lissa

Chapter eight

Alissa

To say that I was surprised to see Malik at Walmart would be an understatement. I hadn't seen or heard from him since that time I offended him about using his daughter to get my attention. As soon as I said those words, I could've shoved my foot in my mouth. Mainly because I saw first- hand just how much he loved his daughters. I should've never said that to him. So, for the past six months, I had been keeping busy with work, so I hadn't had time to think about Malik. I had wondered about his baby girl, but I wasn't going to call him.

So, when he approached me in Walmart and gave me a hug, I was shocked. Once we hugged and my body began to tingle, I got excited. He said he still had my number and invited me to his place, so of course I accepted. I couldn't wait to see his little girl. I was anxious to see how she was and how he was doing. I wanted to see where he lived also. You could tell a lot about someone from where they lived and how they kept up their space.

When I pulled into the driveway attached to the address that Malik had given me, I had a feeling I was in the wrong damn driveway. The house was huge. I went to the door and rang the bell expecting for someone else to answer it. But then Malik and Riley answered, and I was floored. Riley was a little cool when we first saw each other again, but then she remembered who I was. The warm little hug she gave me melted my heart. That along with the hug her dad gave me had me like a big old glob of mush.

Once the tour was over, Malik ordered food. We sat on the sofa and watched the movie. When Riley leaned her little head against my shoulder, I put my arm around her. She rested her head against my boob and fell asleep. After the movie was over, Malik picked her up and brought her to bed. I picked up the food boxes and plates to take into the kitchen. I tossed the trash and put the plates in the dishwasher. Then I went to get Malik's empty beer bottle, Riley's empty drink cup and my glass. I tossed the beer bottle and rinsed the cup Riley had her Kool-Aid in before I put it in the dishwasher.

Malik poured another glass of wine for me and some Remy for him and we went back to the living room. When he started stroking my bare thigh with his fingertip, I almost jumped out of my skin. As I stared deep into his hungry eyes, I felt a little light headed. Those hazel eyes of his had me in a trance.

"I wanna kiss you so bad right now," he said in a husky whisper.

"Are you waiting for permission?" I asked.

Hell, I wanted him to kiss me, but I wasn't the type of woman to throw myself at a man. No matter how sexy he was.

"Well, I know you got that lil feisty attitude and shit. I ain't trying to get my ass smacked the fuck out!" Malik said as he cracked up laughing, which made me laugh.

"You can rest assured that if you kiss me, I won't smack you."

He leaned in and pressed his lips to mine. Now, I didn't feel fireworks, but my lips did sizzle. It almost felt as if I had locked lips with a taser, but I couldn't stop myself. I almost spilled my wine in his lap, so I pulled away quickly. Of course, that sent the wrong signals to him.

"I'm sorry!" he apologized.

I downed the rest of my wine without saying anything. Once I had that extra bit of confidence from the alcohol, I took his drink from him and started kissing him again. Fuck what I said about not wanting to throw myself at this man. I couldn't help myself. The kiss between us deepened as his hands caressed my body. When he laid me on the sofa and climbed on top of me, I had to stop this.

"Okay, as good as this feels I can't do this..." I said.

I mean, what if Riley walked in on us. This wouldn't be appropriate for a six- year old to see. "I'm sorry," he said. "I didn't mean to get carried away like that."

"It's not that. I mean, number one, I'm not used to doing this on the first date."

"I know. You're a good girl."

"I really am."

"I know."

"Second, what if Riley walks in on us? The last thing I want is for your little girl to walk in on the two of us in a compromising position," I said.

"You're absolutely right. I don't know what I was thinking."

"You weren't," I chuckled.

He leaned in and kissed me again. The kiss deepened once again, but then he pulled away. He stood up and reached his hand out to me. I was confused because I thought maybe he was getting ready to throw me out. I put my hand in his and he pulled me up. He held me close before leaning his head forward and kissing me again. This man had my toes curling at this point.

"I want you to do me a favor," he said as he stared into my soul with his piercing eyes.

"What?" I asked weakly.

"I know you're a good girl and all, but I want you to throw caution to the wind."

"What does that mean?"

"I want you to spend the night with me. Shit, spend the weekend with me and Riley," he offered.

"And then what? What's going to happen after the weekend is over?" I asked.

"I really like you Alissa. I like you a lot. You're beautiful, smart, caring and you care a lot about my little girl. That means more to me than anything. I can't say what will happen after this weekend, but I've been single for a while now. If this takes us to a relationship, then I'd like to explore that. So, would you be open to that?"

"I'm open to it."

"So, will you spend the weekend with us?"

My nerves were so bad right now because I didn't know how to answer that. I didn't want to make the wrong decision. Never in my life had I slept with a man after the first night. But I hadn't seen this man in a while and feeling the way that I was feeling right now, I didn't want to leave him. I decided to do what he asked me to do and throw caution to the wind.

A Thug's Romance for Valentine's Day

"Yes," I said.

This man actually picked me up off my feet with my legs wrapped around his waist and walked me towards his bedroom. His hands felt good on my ass and his tongue felt amazing in my mouth. I was definitely nervous about taking this step with him, especially because we didn't know each other that well. But what I knew of him let me know that he was a good man.

When we got in his bedroom, he placed my feet on the floor and shut the door. He clicked the lock in place and my eyes widened. What if Riley woke up? How is she going to reach him if the door is locked?

"Riley sleeps straight through the night," he said as if he could read my mind.

"But what if she doesn't?"

"She always does. Stop worrying," he said. "If it'll make you feel better, I can unlock it and just let her walk in on us."

I walked over to him and put my arms around his waist. "Can we just lay in bed and hold each other? Would that be okay with you?" I asked.

"Yea, sure."

"I just don't want us to rush into something and I'll have regrets in the morning," I said.

I was really struggling with having sex with him on the first night. I just didn't want him to lose respect for me by doing that. So, the two of us got comfortable... him in his boxers and a wifebeater and me in one of his oversized t-shirts. We climbed in the huge California King bed and met up in the middle. He wrapped his arm around me and held me close. Not long after, we were both sleeping.

The next morning, I woke up still wrapped in his arms. It felt so good because Maverick never held me all night. He would hold me until I fell asleep, but then afterward, he would release me and turn his back towards me. We would always wake up in the morning in total opposite positions... unless he wanted to have sex. But Malik was different. He held me in his arms the entire night and never once put the moves on me.

I kissed his lips softly as I heard tiny knocks on the bedroom door. "Malik," I whispered as I nudged him lightly. "Malik."

He didn't even budge, so I slipped out of the bed and went to the door. I opened it and Riley looked up at me with a surprised expression on her little face. "Lissa you're still here!" she said happily as she reached for me.

I picked her up and realized how heavy she had gotten over the past six months. I shut the door to Malik's bedroom and headed to the kitchen with Riley.

"Are you hungry?" I asked.

"Yea."

"You wanna help me cook breakfast for us and daddy?"

"Yeaaaaaa!" She was so excited she was clapping.

"Okay, what do you wanna eat?"

"Daddy likes omelets."

"And what do you like?"

"I like omelets too," she said.

"So, let's see if daddy has stuff in the fridge for omelets," I said as I opened the refrigerator.

I pulled out the carton of eggs, some bacon, ham and cheese. Then I grabbed the butter and frying pan. "Do you want grits or biscuits?" I asked Riley.

"Can we have toast?" she asked.

"Of course."

So, she sat on the counter while I whipped up three bacon, cheese and ham omelets. Once I was done with those, I placed some slices of white bread in the toaster. When the toast popped up, I let Riley spread the butter. I poured three glasses of orange juice and then set the plates and juice glasses on the table, with Riley's help of course. When we were done, we went to wake her dad.

The two of us tiptoed quietly into the room and then climbed in the bed to wake Malik.

"Daddy! Daddy! Daddy wake up!" Riley called out as she and I nudged her father.

He slowly opened his eyes and tried to focus. He looked at the two of us before a smile graced his face. "What are you two up to?" Malik asked.

"We made breakfast daddy! C'mon!" Riley called as she pulled his left arm.

"Okay, okay!" Malik said as the three of us climbed out of bed.

We walked down the hallway and into the dining room. Malik's face lit up as he looked at the food and juice. "You did this?" he asked me as he walked over to me.

"No, me and Riley did it, didn't we sweetie?" I asked her.

"Yeaaaa!" she yelled happily.

He picked Riley up and kissed her cheek before he bent his head to kiss me on the lips. Riley's little face was priceless when she saw her dad kiss me. It was too cute.

"Thank you both so much," Malik said.

We all sat down to eat. While we ate, we spoke about a lot of different things. Mostly Riley rambled on about how excited she was that I was still here. When Malik told her that I would be staying the weekend, she was ecstatic.

"Are you and Lissa boyfriend and girlfriend now?" Riley asked.

I looked at Malik because I wasn't sure how to answer that question.

"Well, Alissa and I like each other very much. So, I guess you could say that we're boyfriend and girlfriend. Are you okay with that?" Malik asked his little girl.

"Yes, I like Lissa!" Riley said as she smiled at me.

"Good. I'm glad to hear that because I'd like for Alissa to be around for a long time," Malik said as he stared at me.

The look he was giving me sent chills up and down my spine. I literally felt chills down to my toes. "I gotta go home and get some clothes," I said.

"That's cool. I can take you," he offered.

"Are you sure? Because I can drive myself and come back."

"It's cool. Me and Riley would be happy to take you. You can just park your car in the garage."

"Okay."

When I first met Malik, I didn't know what to think about him. Then when I saw him at the hospital, my heart broke for him. Never would I have imagined we'd be sitting here together with his daughter discussing a relationship. It was crazy, but it felt good. After breakfast, I went with Riley to pick out something to wear while Malik took a shower. When he was done getting dressed, we all climbed into his truck and he drove me to my apartment to shower and get clothes. I decided to bring my nurse's uniform just in case I stayed until Monday.

We were walking out of my apartment when Maverick appeared on my walkway. I wasn't going to entertain this bullshit, especially not in front of Malik and Riley.

"Hey Alissa, can we talk?" Maverick asked.

"NO!" I responded as I walked pass him.

Malik unlocked the doors and I opened the passenger's side door to climb in while he strapped Riley in her seat. "I know I fucked up, but I really need to talk to you."

"I have nothing to say to you. Go home to your wife!" I said before I shut the door.

Malik climbed in the driver's seat and started the truck. He backed out of the spot and we headed back to his house. I knew he probably had questions about who Maverick was, but I was glad he didn't say anything about it in front of Riley. The ride to his house was quiet. I was sure he was wondering why my ex had shown up on my doorstep. I wondered if he even remembered him from the parking lot on Valentine's Day when I was upset.

My head was definitely reeling. Like why the hell did Maverick show up at my place. What the hell did he want? I hadn't heard from him since I busted him and his new wife that day, so what the hell did he want now?

"You aight?" Malik asked as he touched my thigh.

A jolt of static electricity caused my body to quiver. As quick as he pulled his hand away, I was sure he felt it too. "Yea, I'm fine. Just thinking about what we're going to do today," I lied.

"What would you like to do?"

"I think we should do something that Riley wants to do."

"That's a good idea. Riley, what do you wanna do today?" Malik asked as he peered at his little girl in the rearview mirror.

"Uhm, can we go to the water park?" Riley asked.

"To Schlitterbahn?" Malik probed.

Riley nodded her head profusely. Malik looked over at me and asked, "So, you feel like taking a ride to Galveston?"

"Sure, but I didn't pack a swimsuit."

"We can swing by the mall and you can pick one up real quick," Malik suggested.

"Are you sure? I don't want to put you through too much trouble," I said.

"It's cool. We aren't that far from the mall anyway, unless you prefer to get one on the way to Galveston."

"No, we can stop by the mall. I can easily find one at Macy's and be in and out," I said.

"Cool. Okay baby, we have to stop by the mall so Alissa can get a swimsuit, then we'll head home and get you ready. Okay," he asked.

"Okay. I love the water park!" Riley said.

"She hasn't been this excited in a long time. I think it's cuz of you," Malik said as he reached for my hand.

He linked his fingers through mine and smiled. "I think you're giving me too much credit."

"Nah, I think I'm giving you the right amount of credit. The look on my child's face right now says it all and it means the world to me to see her this happy."

He pulled into the mall parking lot a short time later, our fingers still locked together. Once he found a parking spot, we got out of the truck and headed inside Macy's. He held my hand and I held Riley's hand as we made our way to the swimsuit section of the women's department. As I browsed through the swimsuits trying to find the right one, I heard Malik blow out an exasperated breath. I looked over at him to see the happy look that was just on his face was no longer there. I quickly grabbed a swimsuit in my size because it seemed like something was about to pop off.

I just didn't realize the extent of it all would be as bad as it was.

"Baby daddy, is that you?" I looked up to see a pregnant female walking towards us.

The words 'baby daddy' coming from the mouth of a pregnant woman caught me off guard. Malik hadn't mentioned to me that he was expecting a baby with anyone. If he was, I couldn't fault him for any of it because it happened before we got together. However, if he knew and was hiding it from me, that was a totally different thing.

"Look at this bitch!" he said as he shook his head. "Did you find something?"

I nodded my head and lifted up the suit. He grabbed my hand and I took Riley's as we headed to a register to check out.

"Baby daddy I know you see me!" the woman called out.

We kept walking until we got to the register. I placed the swimsuit on the counter and Malik paid for it. "I know you did not just pay for the new bitch's shit when you ain't even been giving me money for our baby!" the woman said.

"Malik, I know she didn't just call me a bitch!" I said to him in a hushed tone because I didn't want to scare Riley.

"Just ignore her bae. That bitch is crazy!"

The three of us walked out the door, but the woman continued to follow us. Once we got to the truck, Malik strapped Riley in her seat, and I climbed in the front seat. Before he could climb in the driver's seat, the woman was on him.

"You can't ignore me forever Bishop!"

"Bitch get the fuck out of my face!" Malik said angrily.

"Oh, so now I'm a bitch? The mother of your child..."

"Bitch you ain't the mother of my child! We had sex ONCE and I strapped up!" Malik fussed. "You better go find yo real baby daddy and get the fuck outta my face!"

"This is your baby..."

"Girl get on with that shit! I WILL NEVER ACCEPT THAT YOUR KID IS MINE!! PERIODT!!"

I could tell how angry he was and wanted to get out the truck and slap that bitch for making him act this way in front of Riley. After everything this little girl had been through, this was something she didn't need.

"NOW, GET THE FUCK AWAY FROM MY TRUCK BEFORE I POP YO ASS!!"

"Alright, but once this baby is born, YOU GON' HAVE TO ACCEPT HIM!!"

"I AIN'T ACCEPTING SHIT THAT AIN'T MINE!!" Malik said.

"YOU ACCEPTED OLIVIA AND SHE WASN'T YOURS!!" the woman hollered.

"What the fuck did you say?"

"YOU HEARD ME!! OLIVIA WASN'T YOURS BUT YOU STILL TOOK CARE OF HER LIKE SHE WAS!!"

I jumped out the truck because I knew at that point Malik was about to lose it. I rushed over to the other side and pushed the woman out the way to open the truck door.

"BITCH I KNOW YOU DIDN'T JUST PUSH ME!!" the woman said from behind me.

"Malik get in the truck!" I urged.

He looked at me with tears threatening to fall. I didn't know if it was from anger or sorrow for the little girl he lost, but this bitch had really opened up a huge can of worms. He climbed in the truck and looked down at me. I turned to face the woman who looked like she wanted to jump on me.

"Let me tell you something, I don't know what your business is with Malik and I don't care. But that little girl in the back seat has been through enough these past few months. The last thing she needs is for you to attack her dad while she's sitting right there…"

"Bitch fuck you! You don't even know that nigga. Calling him Malik and shit! Call him Bishop like the rest of us who know him for who he really is!" she spewed.

"If you really knew me, you would carry yo ass on. That is if you know what I'm capable of," he said from behind me.

The woman looked at him and all that rage she had was replaced with fear. Without another word, she rushed off like her draws were flaming. I went around to the passenger's side and got in.

"Are you okay?" I asked.

"No, I'm not okay."

"Who was that?"

He didn't respond as he turned to face Riley. "Baby are you okay?" he asked.

She nodded her head, but I could tell she was shaken. "Daddy why did Kiki yell at you?"

"I don't know baby girl. I think Kiki had too much coffee or something!" Malik said.

That caused Riley to laugh a little. "Yea, way too much coffee. Can we go to the water park now?" Riley asked.

I could tell that Malik didn't really want to go anymore. He looked like he wanted to hurt someone, probably his baby mama after what he had just heard. But he plastered a fake smile on his face and said, "Sure. Let's go home and change and grab some towels. Then we can be on our way."

"Are you sure?" I asked.

"My daughter wants to go to the water park. It ain't about me, it's about her."

In that moment, regardless of everything I had heard, I wanted to jump on his lap and give him the business. But that wasn't going to happen anytime soon. I think Malik and I needed to have a serious talk when we got back though. If we were really going to try and make this work, we had to put all our cards on the table.

And that meant everything...

Chapter nine

Kiki

Bishop must have me fucked up or something. How the hell he gon' tell me that he ain't accepting my baby as his, but he accepted Priscilla's? What made that bitch so damn special? He didn't even ask for a paternity test when she said she was pregnant, even though they were together off and on during that time. He just assumed that she was telling the truth, but guess what? That bitch lied! Olivia wasn't Bishop's daughter. Riley was, but not Olivia. I wondered if I should give Priscilla the heads up that I let the cat out of the bag on that one. I knew Bishop was probably on his way over to her place right now. Lord I'd love to be a fly on the wall for that shit.

And who the hell was the new bitch? Where the fuck did she come from? She looked familiar but I couldn't place where I had seen her at. I wondered if Priscilla knew about her and that she was spending time with Riley. She seemed pretty close to Bishop and her concern for Riley let me know that she had known them for a while. Then it dawned on me where I had seen her before. She was at Olivia's funeral.

I wondered who the hell she was though with her short ass. If it wasn't for the fact that I was pregnant, I would've cleaned the parking lot with her ass. In any case, I think it was time for me and Priscilla to have a chat. Maybe my baby wasn't for Bishop. Maybe Jason was my baby daddy. But I was going to stick to the story of Bishop being the baby daddy. Hell, if he took care of Olivia's lil ass, he could take care of my child. I called Priscilla on the way to her house just to make sure she was there.

That bitch was always in the streets when Bishop had their daughter. I haven't been hanging with her and Bailey since I got pregnant. Hell, I hadn't even mentioned my pregnancy to them. But that was all about to change.

"Hello."

"Hey, are you home?"

"Yea, why?"

"Cuz I'm coming over there. We have some things to discuss," I informed her.

"What things Kiki?"

"I'll tell you when I get there. You might wanna call Bailey to come over. Some of this shit might come as a surprise to you," I said.

"Bailey is at work."

"Oh, well, I guess it'll be just me and you then."

"I guess so. But what is this about?"

"I'll tell you when I see you. I shouldn't be too long," I said.

"Well, you need to hurry up because I have a date tonight."

"A date or a dick appointment?"

"Whatever it is, it ain't no business of yours!"

"Damn bitch! I thought we were friends," I clowned.

"Hurry the hell up!" Priscilla said before hanging the phone up in my face.

"That bitch rude as fuck, but I got something fa that ass!" I said as I laughed and rubbed my belly. "You're my little meal ticket baby. I'ma make sure Bishop takes very good care of us."

I arrived at Priscilla's house a half hour later after bobbing and weaving through traffic like a Nascar driver. I hate when they shut these damn roads down on weekends to improve them. It just makes it harder for people to get to their damn destinations. I pulled into Priscilla's driveway and shut off the engine. I walked up to the front door and rang the bell.

She opened the door and her mouth fell open. I walked pass her and went straight to the living room. I heard her shut the door and follow behind me.

"So, this is why we haven't seen you in three months. Bitch I didn't know you were pregnant!" Priscilla said obviously in shock.

"I tried to keep this to myself as long as I could, but I need your help."

"What do you need my help with?" she asked.

"So, when you told Bishop you were having Olivia and you knew she wasn't his, what did you say?" I asked.

Her facial expression hardened all of a sudden. "Bitch what?"

"I wanna know how you got Bishop to accept a child that you knew wasn't his."

"Bitch if you wasn't pregnant right now, I would mop the flo' witcho crusty ass! Get the fuck outta my house Kiki!!" Priscilla fussed as she walked towards the front door. "I knew your ass was triflin' but didn't know you would stoop to this level!"

I waddled behind her because I needed her to listen to me.

"I'm not trying to upset you Priscilla..."

"Bitch you're a damn lie! I just lost my daughter six months ago and you come at me with this bullshit!"

"First of all, those kids ain't been nothing but meal tickets for you! I'm just trying to cash in on mine," I said as I rubbed my belly.

She turned to face me with a look on her face that said 1,000 words.

"What the fuck are you trying to say? That you're pregnant for Bishop?"

"No! He used a condom that night!"

"Bitch, you slept with my baby daddy?!" Priscilla asked.

"Uh, you think I'd be standing here saying I did if I didn't?"

WHAP!

That bitch had the nerve to slap me across the face. That shit hurt too. I rubbed the left side of my cheek as the burn set in. My face felt like it was on fire.

"I always knew you were a disrespectful bitch, but I never thought you would go this far!"

"Shit, that ain't even the half of it. I saw Bishop and his new bitch today..."

"What? New bitch? That's not true. Bishop has Riley this weekend..."

"Yep, I saw her too. They were in Macy's."

All the color seemed to drain from her face at that point. "Get out Kiki!" she said as she opened the door.

"Okay. I'll leave," I said as I walked towards the door. As I stopped in her personal space, I turned to her and smiled. "I understand you're upset, but shit is about to hit the fan for you, so I wanted to give you a warning."

"What the fuck are you talking about Kiki?"

"I kinda told him that Olivia wasn't his..."

"YOU DID WHAT?!"

"He and I were arguing and it sorta slipped out!" I said as I shrugged my shoulders.

"GET OUT!!"

"Priscilla..."

"GET THE FUCK OUTTA MY HOUSE KIKI!!" Priscilla yelled angrily. That bitch looked like a mad dog, so maybe, just maybe, I took it a little too far.

"Pris..."

"I SWEAR TO YOU AND THE LORD ABOVE THAT IF YOU DON'T GET THE FUCK OUT OF MY HOUSE RIGHT NOW, I'LL THROW YOU OUT!! And you know the law will be on my fuckin' side!" she seethed through clenched teeth.

Damn! She mad mad! Without saying another word, I walked out the door. She slammed it behind me closing not only the door to her house, but the door to our friendship as well. I didn't care though. At the end of the day, Bishop was going to take care of my child the same way he took care of Priscilla's little bastard.

"Aw damn!"

I probably shouldn't have said that about the little girl since she was no longer here. I looked up at the roof of my car and said a quick prayer for God to forgive me for my wayward tongue. Shit, sometimes I said shit that surprised me just as much as it did everyone else.

I hoped the shit that I said today didn't come back to bite me in the ass...

Chapter ten

Priscilla

No, this bitch did not just come to my house to tell me she had fucked up my whole life. I knew she didn't tell Bishop that Olivia wasn't his. She had to be lying about that part because if she had told him, his ass would've been here before her. How could I have trusted her? How could I have thought that ho' was my friend? I called Bishop not only to see where his head was at, but to find out if he had some random bitch around my daughter. The nerve of him if he did.

I wasn't going to jump to conclusions with him because Kiki could have been lying to piss me off. Shit, I was already pissed off. I picked up my phone and called Bishop, but he didn't answer. I called him back a second time and he still didn't respond. I knew that Kiki had to be lying about telling him about Olivia because if she had told him, he would've answered that phone and chewed me out. I wanted to know who that bitch was that he was hanging out with, if there even was a bitch.

I called Bailey because I needed to know if she knew about Kiki's pregnancy and her obvious infatuation with Bishop. She answered on the third ring.

"Hey girl, what's going on?" Bailey answered.

"I'm sorry to bother you at work, but I really need to talk to you. Are you busy?"

"Not at the moment. What's up?"

"You will never guess who just left my house..."

"You're right, I can't guess because too many people know where you live," she clowned.

I couldn't even laugh at her joke because this shit with Kiki had me way too hot.

"Well, Kiki just left my house!"

"For real? I ain't seen that bitch in months. What did she want?"

"She's pregnant..."

"Pregnant? For who... Jason's no good ass again?" Bailey asked.

"She claims she's pregnant by my baby daddy..."

All of a sudden, Bailey started coughing and choking on the other end of the phone. I heard her sipping on some water as she tried to calm herself. "Are you okay?"

"I'm fine. Did you say Kiki said that Bishop is her baby's daddy?"

"Yes, that's what I said!"

"Well, what kind of shit is that? How the fuck she get him to sleep with her?"

"I don't know, but she came in here on some bullshit. She was asking me what I told him when I told him I was pregnant with Olivia..."

"What you told him? What the hell she means what you told him?"

"Because Olivia wasn't his! She asked how I broke the news of the pregnancy to him knowing Olivia wasn't his!" I cried.

"Well, there ya go! Her kid ain't his either!" Bailey said.

"Bailey, she said she told him..."

"Told him what?"

"That Olivia wasn't his!"

"I know you fucking lying to me right now!" Bailey said.

"I think she was lying to me. You know if she had told Bishop that shit, his ass would've been over here all up in my damn face! I tried calling him twice, but he didn't answer my calls."

"Then she has to be lying. Because like you said, if she had told him, he would've been over there right now. I can't believe Kiki did that shit though. She broke the damn girl's code," Bailey said.

"That bitch could never be in my space again! I ain't going to try and stop you from being her friend, but I am done with her ass!" I said.

"With good reason. What the hell was she thinking?"

"She wasn't. That's not all she told me."

"Whew chile! I don't think I could take anymore," Bailey expressed.

"She said Bishop has a new bitch."

"What?"

"Yea, she said she saw them at the mall!"

"Well, you two aren't together, so..."

"That doesn't mean I want some random bitch around my daughter!" I fumed.

"Maybe she's not a random bitch. Maybe she's someone he really cares about," Bailey argued.

"Well, regardless of the fact, he didn't tell me he would have another bitch around my baby!"

"Not to side with him, but do you tell him when you have other dudes around Riley? Just asking because if you two are going to co-parent this little girl after everything she's been through, y'all have to learn to communicate. You can't be going all LOCO on him in front of your daughter. She needs to see that her parents are doing what's best for her and that means y'all can't be trippin'!" Bailey said. "Now, I have to get back to work. I have a little bit of paperwork left to finish, but I'll come by when I get off."

"Thanks for listening Bailey."

"That's what friends are for."

"I'm glad to know I have at least one real one left," I said.

"Always."

We ended the call and I tried calling Bishop again. He still didn't answer. I figured by now that Kiki probably lied about telling him about Olivia's paternity.

That evil bitch!

She pretended to be my friend all this fucking time just to get Bishop.

"That jealous muthafucka!" I fumed.

I couldn't believe I trusted that bitch. Why didn't I see through her shit? I mean, she was always talking about if she were me and what she would do differently. She was always making comments about what she would do if Bishop were her man. How the hell did she get him to sleep with her anyway?

I wasn't worried about her carrying Bishop's baby because I knew he had used a condom if they had slept together. If he did sleep with Kiki when he knew we were friends, he was wrong too. I wondered how she got him in bed though. That shit right there would drive me crazy if I let it so instead of worry about what might and might not have happened, I went to the fridge and grabbed a bottle of wine. Then I thought about something that would make me feel better than wine.

"Wassup?" Came the deep voice on the other end of the line.

"I need you. Can you come over?"

"On my way," he said before he hung up.

I smiled just thinking about the dick I was about to get to put me in a better mood. I rushed to the bathroom to take a quick shower. I wanted to smell good and fresh by the time he came by. I lathered myself with vanilla and coconut body scrub. Then I rinsed it off and got out. By the time I had thrown on a rob, he was ringing my doorbell.

I couldn't get to the door fast enough. I pulled it back and his eyes lit up like a Christmas tree. I saw the hungry look in them as I backed up to let him in. He quickly closed and locked the door before closing the space between us. He threw me up against the wall and kissed me hard and passionate. I held onto him as he opened my robe. His fingers immediately invaded my hot juice box. I moaned as he stuffed his fingers in and out of me before putting his fingers in his mouth. I smiled as he licked the juices from his fingers.

I quickly dropped to my knees and took his dick out of his grey sweatpants. I marveled at the length and width of his dick. I couldn't wait to get it inside me. I wrapped my lips around it in an effort to get it even more erect than it already was. I sucked it and licked it until he was as hard as he could be. He kicked off his shoes and pants and lifted me up. He carried me to the sofa and climbed on top of me.

His dick immediately found its way inside me. "Fuck me!" I cried as he pummeled his dick inside me. "Sssss!"

He covered my lips with his for a passionate kiss as I wrapped my legs around his waist. That shit felt so good. His dick wasn't better than Bishop's dick, but it was still good as hell. He placed my legs in the crooks of his arms and went inside deeper. My body shuddered as my first orgasm came to the surface.

"Turn over," he said huskily.

Shit, he ain't had to tell me twice. I quickly turned over as soon as he pulled out. He got behind me and slammed into the back of me full force. He hit my G-spot so hard, I found myself biting down on the arm of the sofa. After several minutes, he finally released, and I collapsed on my stomach. He smacked my ass before he went to put his boxers and pants on.

"Whew!" I blew out an exasperated breath.

"You got some good pussy!"

"Shit, you got some good dick!"

"Aye sit up though. I need to talk to you about something," he said as he smacked my backside again.

The last thing I wanted to do was sit up after a dick down like I had just received, but I wanted to know what was up with him. "What's going on?" I asked as I sat next to him.

"When you gon' tell Bishop about us?"

"What do you mean?"

"I mean, when are you going to tell Bishop about us?"

"To be honest Tony, I had no intentions on telling Bishop anything about what we've been doing."

"Why not?"

"Because you're his boy. I'm not trying to start no static between y'all because you broke the bro code," I said.

"You let me worry about that."

"I don't want him to know!"

"So, you just wanna continue to use me behind closed doors?"

"If that's what you think I'm doing with you, we must be using each other. I mean, you're getting just as much out of this as I am."

"Maybe it's just me, but I thought you were feeling me."

"I guess, but I'm not feeling you enough to piss Bishop off," I said as I stood up from the sofa.

"See, now you trippin'!" Tony said.

I thought because he and Bishop were boys, he would understand why we had to keep this shit on the hush. I mean, we had been sleeping together for the past three months. Not once did he mention that he wanted people to know about us. This relationship was supposed to be on the hush.

"How? How am I tripping? When we got involved, we agreed to keep this a secret. We agreed to keep it between the two of us. I just don't understand why you wanna ruin things now!"

"I'm just tired being a closet nigga!"

"Okay, well, how about we just end this now?! How about that?"

"What? So, you're saying that you would rather end things between us than instead of tell Bishop?"

"YES!! That's exactly what I'm saying!" I said.

"Wow That's bullshit!"

"To you it's bullshit, but to me it could ruin my damn life!"

"Why? Cuz Bishop won't pay you all the money he's been paying you?" Tony asked angrily. "Shit, I can take care of you and Riley! I got money!"

"You ain't got half the money Bishop has! He's the king, you're only a servant!"

"A servant?! You know what Priscilla? Fuck you and lose my fuckin' number!"

He stuck his feet in his shoes and headed for the door.

"Tony!" I called before he walked out. He turned to face me with an angry look on his face. "Please don't tell Bishop!"

"Kiss my ass!" Tony said before he walked out and slammed the door.

"Dammit!!" I cussed at myself.

Bishop was going to kill us if he found out we had been sleeping together.

Chapter eleven

Bishop

The morning started off ridiculously crazy and with so much drama, I just knew Alissa was going to be done with my black ass. But surprisingly, we still went to Galveston and had a great time with Riley. My little girl had the time of her life. I hadn't seen her laugh that much in a long time. She had so much fun that she crashed out in the back seat the whole way home. There were some things I wanted to discuss with Alissa pertaining to today's events, but I wasn't going to do it while heading home. I didn't want to risk Riley waking up and hearing anything that didn't involve her.

So, once we got back to my place, I pulled into the garage and got out my sleeping child. She woke up as soon as I stepped inside the house. "I'm glad you're awake. You need to take a bath before you eat and go to bed."

"Okay daddy. Can Lissa give me a bath?" Riley asked.

I turned to Alissa who had a huge smile on her face. "Would you mind?"

"Not at all," she said. "C'mon baby."

Riley jumped into her arms as they headed to her room. A few minutes later, I heard the water running in my bathroom. I used that time to call Priscilla's ass. Before the phone could ring, I hung up. This was a conversation that would be better to have in person. That way I could tell if she was lying or not. As a matter of fact, I had to find that shit out now or I wouldn't be able to sleep. I went to the bathroom and told Alissa I had somewhere to go.

"Would you mind watching her for me?"

"Not at all."

"I won't be long," I said.

"Okay." She had a confused expression on her face, but I'd explain it all to her once I got back.

I drove the half hour distance to Priscilla's house and got the shock of my life when I arrived. Please tell me why when I turned down her street, I saw my boy Tony's whip in her driveway. I passed the driveway up and parked a couple of houses down just to see how long it would take for him to come out of her house. It took that nigga about 20 minutes to come busting up out of there with an attitude.

"Humph."

He was so pissed that he didn't even notice my truck when he flew by. I started my truck and turned in her driveway. I didn't know what that nigga was doing over here, but something told me I should've used my key to let myself in. Maybe I would've busted in on them doing something they shouldn't have been doing. I'd find out though because he just left, so I knew she was probably about to jump in the shower. I didn't use my key because if she was about to jump in the shower, I wanted her to come get the door first. So, I rang the doorbell.

A couple of seconds later, she answered the door in a robe.

"Did you forget someth… oh, Bishop. Wh-wh-wh-what are you doing here?" she asked nervously.

I walked pass her and waited for her to shut the door.

"A better question would be what the fuck was Tony doing here?" I asked.

"Huh? What are you talking about?"

"Just what the fuck I said! I just saw that nigga leave here! So, what the fuck was he doing here?"

"N-n-n-n-n-nothing! He wasn't doing nothing!"

"How long you been fucking Tony?" I asked.

"Wh-wh-what?"

"You heard me bitch! How long you been fuckin' Tony?!"

"Why you calling me out my name?"

"Is he Olivia's real daddy?" I asked.

I was so mad right now. I mean, I didn't think I could recall a time when I was this fucking upset.

"Uuuuhhh, don't be stupid! You're Olivia's..."

"DON'T YOU FUCKIN' LIE TO ME!!" I yelled as I pointed my finger in her face. "KIKI ALREADY TOLD ME THAT YOU LIED ABOUT ME BEING OLIVIA'S DAD!!"

"And you believed her?"

"You damn right!"

"Why?"

"Tony just left here and your house smells like pussy! I know y'all was fuckin' up in here and you got the nerve to ask me why?!" I asked angrily.

"Bishop it ain't..."

"Don't you fuckin' tell me it ain't what I think!" I said as I walked over to her and opened her robe. Just as I thought, she was butt ass naked under it. "See, I knew you was a nasty triflin' ass woman! People told me about you before I started fuckin' witchu and I still did it! I shoulda listened!"

She closed her robe and looked at me. "Wow! You have a lot of nerve coming at me like that Bishop when you got Kiki's ass pregnant!!"

"What?"

"Yea, she came by here today to let me know about y'all baby that she was having!"

"Okay, first of all, that ain't my fuckin' kid! I fucked that ho' once a long time ago and with a condom. So, don't even try it!"

"You still slept with her... knowing we were friends!"

"That bitch wasn't your friend! She been trying to fuck with me, and that night she came by without any fuckin' clothes on, I gave her what she wanted. But I wasn't stupid enough not to strap up, so she better go find her real baby daddy!" I said. "You, on the other hand, told me that Olivia was mine. Why did you lie?"

"Bishop..."

"I asked you a question!" I said through clenched teeth.

"Well, let me ask you one. Where's my daughter?"

"She's at my house..."

"With your new bitch Kiki saw you with at the mall? Huh?"

"Maybe. Maybe not!" I said. "This is my weekend, so as long as Riley is safe, I could leave her with who the fuck I wanna leave her with!"

"No, you can't! You can't be leaving our child with some random bitch..."

"Who said she was random?"

"Well, who is she?"

"None of yo fuckin' business!"

"If my daughter is involved, it is my business!"

"Our daughter! Riley is our daughter! Unless you lied to me about her too!"

"Don't be silly Bishop!"

"Silly my ass! Monday I'm taking Riley to the diagnostics lab for a DNA test!"

"Is that really necessary?" Priscilla asked.

"Yes! Not because I'll ever stop being Riley's dad because I won't..."

"Then what's the point?"

"Because you're a liar! I swear though that if you've been lying to me about Riley being my kid... I swear to God!" I didn't finish it because she already knew.

"Bishop, Riley is your daughter!"

"Was Olivia? Huh? Was Olivia my blood daughter?" I asked.

"Bishop..."

"Just tell me the damn truth Priscilla!"

"NO! Alright!" she finally admitted.

Tears sprung to my eyes at the thought that Olivia wasn't my blood daughter. I had just stopped grieving over her death and now I felt like I was grieving all over again. Like damn! When was a nigga gon' catch a break?

I turned to leave her house because if I didn't, I'd probably choke that bitch. "Bishop..."

A Thug's Romance for Valentine's Day

I turned with my hand up to stop her from saying anything else.

"Please don't say shit else to me right now!" I said. "I'm trying my best to walk out of here right now without choking yo ass!"

"I'm sorry," she said through trembling lips as tears rained down her cheeks.

I didn't respond because I was too choked up. I just turned and walked out the door, slamming it behind me. I couldn't believe that bitch had lied to me that way. She had looked me dead in the eyes and told me Olivia was my daughter. I didn't doubt her because we already had Riley and I had been sleeping with her around that time. I just didn't know she was sleeping with another nigga.

I backed out of her driveway and sped off. That bitch! Tears streamed down my face like a kid who had been told he couldn't have a toy in the toy store. I made it home and Alissa was waiting up for me. She took one look at me and held her arms out to me. I immediately went into them and held her as I cried some more.

"She wasn't mine bae!" I cried. "My little girl wasn't mine!"

"Yes, she was Malik! Olivia was your little girl since birth. Don't let the fact that your blood wasn't running through her veins change the way you saw her. I watched you grieve and mourn for your daughter in a way that only a parent could do! She was your child!" Alissa said.

She was right. I had been raising Olivia since day one. If that didn't make me her daddy, I didn't know what would. After a few minutes, my tears subsided.

"I'm gonna go take a shower," I said.

"Okay. Riley is asleep, so I'll wait for you in the bedroom if that's okay," she said.

I kissed her soft lips. "Yea, it's fine. Thank you for being here."

"You're welcome."

She followed me to the bedroom, and I got a pair of boxers and a t-shirt from the drawer.

She apparently had taken a shower already because she was comfortably dressed in some boy shorts and a t-shirt. I headed to the bathroom and turned the water on. While the water warmed up, I went and sat on the toilet. My stomach had been bubbling since earlier, so I knew as soon as I sat down, it was going to blow. Just as I knew it would, my ass exploded once I sat down on the toilet. I didn't have time to worry about the smell or if Alissa could hear me farting. All I wanted was some relief.

Once I was done, I wiped my ass and walked in the shower stall. I scrubbed and lathered and scrubbed some more. I finally exited the shower about 20 minutes later.

I dried myself off and put on some lotion and deodorant. I finally walked back into the bedroom and joined Alissa in the bed.

"Are you okay?" she asked.

"I will be."

"What happened? Where'd you go?"

"I had to go see my baby mama..."

"About what that chick at the mall told you?"

I nodded my head. "She admitted it."

"Admitted what?"

"That Olivia wasn't my daughter."

"But she was your daughter..."

"She wasn't my biolo..."

"It doesn't matter. None of that matters now Malik," Alissa said as she tilted my chin so I could look into her eyes. "Does that make you love her any less now than when she was alive?"

"No."

"Then please don't let that get to you too much. That little girl loved you. You were the only dad who stepped up, claimed her and took care of her. She's gone now, so none of that stuff should even matter right now."

"I know, but it's the fact that she lied to me. Like she knew I wasn't the dad and she still lied to me!" I said.

"I could understand how that would upset you. But please don't let it tarnish the good times and memories you shared with Olivia. When she woke up during the night crying for her dad, you were there. When she hurt herself or made a boo boo, you were there. She was your daughter in every sense of the word and every way that counts. Don't lose sight of that," she said.

"Thanks for being here. I think if you weren't, I'd be drowning my sorrows in alcohol."

"Please don't do that. I still have questions for you."

Shit, I expected her to have questions after everything that transpired today.

"Shoot!"

"Who was that girl at the mall?"

"One of Priscilla's "besties"."

"Wow! And you slept with her?"

"Once!" I said as I raised my finger. "My daughter had just died, and I was in my feelings. She came over here butt naked with a coat on."

"So, you took her to bed?"

"To bed? Hell naw!" I yelled. "I fucked that ho' on the floor by the front door and from the back with a rubber!"

"Wow!"

"All she got was about five pumps and I wouldn't have given her that if I hadn't been caught up in losing Olivia. That's how I know that ain't my kid!"

"How can you be so sure though?"

"Trust me... that kid ain't mine! That bitch is looking for a come up... period!"

"So, uhm..."

"Uhm what? Ask me whatever you wanna know."

"Whose Bishop?" she asked.

Damn! I was hoping she wouldn't ask that question, but she did.

I inhaled deeply before answering. "Bishop is my street name," I admitted.

"Your street name?"

"Yea, kinda like a nickname."

"Why do you need a street name?"

"Because in case you haven't noticed, I'm a street nigga!" I said.

"So, you sell drugs and stuff..."

"I'm a businessman."

"What businesses do you own?"

"I have a club off the Katy Freeway called Torrential," I said.

"Club Torrential is your club?"

"Yep. The building went on the market a couple of years ago and I scooped it up."

"Wow! I didn't know."

"Now, you do." I leaned against her and inhaled. "You smell good."

"Don't try and change the subject Bishop," she said as she stared at me.

"I like when you call me by my street name," I said as I kissed her neck.

"Stop it!"

I trailed my tongue along her earlobe and felt her body quiver.

"You really want me to stop?" I asked as I turned her face ever so slightly and kissed her lips. She opened her mouth to receive my tongue and the kiss deepened. I trailed my kiss from her mouth to her neck as she moaned softly.

I laid her down on the bed and lifted her shirt. Her perky boobs jumped out in front of me and I began to lick and suck on them, one at a time. She moaned as she ran her fingers through my curly hair. I slid my lips down her stomach, dipping my tongue inside her sweet smelling belly button. I kissed my way all the way to her thighs. My tongue slid up and down the length of her thighs. She shivered as I continued to lick her thighs. When I reached for her shorts, she grabbed my hands.

"I just wanna taste you," I whispered huskily.

"I..."

I covered her mouth with mine because the last thing I needed to hear was her protests. All I needed right now was to feel my dick inside her. I knew she wanted me just as much as I wanted her. I kissed her so deeply, I felt her tonsils. By the time I disconnected my lips from hers and reached for her shorts, she didn't stop me.

I pulled her shorts off and tossed them to the edge of the bed. I parted her lips and drove my tongue up and down the length of her slit. Her body immediately shook, and I could taste her juices. It was clearly obvious that her kitty had been neglected for some time now. I was definitely about to rectify that. As my tongue continued to slid up and down her crevices, I sucked on her clit every couple of seconds. After she erupted in my mouth for the third time, I removed my shirt and boxers and grabbed a condom out of the bedside drawer of the nightstand.

She watched as I slid the condom onto the length of my dick. Then I threw the covers on my bare ass and got between her legs. As I slid my dick up against the opening of her vagina, she jumped slightly. "I'll be gentle," I assured her.

"It's been a while."

"I get it," I said as I kissed her soft lips.

As I pushed my shaft gently inside her, she moaned huskily. I pressed my lips to hers as I held her legs open. "Oh my God!" she cried as she held on to me.

As I rotated my hips against hers, my dick slid in a bit more. After several minutes, my dick was all the way inside her. I didn't want to fuck Alissa because that wasn't what I was looking for right now. I wasn't looking for an easy fuck like my baby mama or her triflin' ass friend. I was looking to possibly build something with this girl, so I was going to take my time with her. I wanted to feel every single part of her pussy and I wanted her to feel every inch of me. She kissed my neck as I drove my dick deeper inside her.

She was definitely a keeper. She had a great sense of humor, a good job, she accepted me and my daughter, and she was level-headed. The fact that she treated Riley so well was what sold me on her as a person. As a man, it was hard to find a woman who wanted to play 'mom' to your kid. Alissa was a natural though. Riley loved her and I could tell that she was just as fond towards Riley.

"Oh my God!" she cried.

Her body started to sputter like an old car on a winter's day. I knew she had cum and hard from the way her eyes were rolling to the back of her head. I kissed her softly and whispered before I rolled onto my back pulling her on top of me. She yelped in surprise, but I quickly covered her lips with mine. I held her hips in place as I thrust upward inside her.

"Mmmmm!" she moaned.

I stuffed her right breast in my mouth and rolled my tongue along her nipple. She moaned and threw her head back. By the time I came, we were both spent. She collapsed beside me as we struggled to get our breathing back to normal. I removed the used condom with a Kleenex tissue and threw it in the trashcan beside my bed. I reached for Alissa and she slid into my arms.

I held her close to me until I heard her softly snoring next to me. I kissed her forehead before I closed my eyes and went to sleep. I wasn't sure where things were going between the two of us, but no matter where it went, she was stuck with me. Alissa was definitely a keeper.

Chapter twelve

Kiki

Three months later...

After a grueling 18 and a half hours, my son had finally entered the world. One of the first people I called was Bishop, but I had the nurse from the hospital make the call.

"What would you like me to say?"

"Just tell him that I had a rough delivery and need him to come down here to help me with our son," I said.

"Okay," she said with a smile.

"Put the phone on speaker. I wanna hear every single word so I can know how to proceed," I said.

I let her see my phone so she could call the right number. "Hello."

"Is this Bishop?"

"Yea, who this?"

"This is a nurse at West Houston Memorial Hospital. I was calling to inform you that Kiosha Parks has given birth to your son..."

"My who?"

"Your son."

"Nah, you got me fucked up! That ain't my fuckin' kid!" Bishop said. "If she had that fuckin' baby, you better ask her for the real baby daddy phone number. Don't fuckin' call this number again!"

With that, he ended the call. The nurse put the phone down and looked at me.

"You didn't even tell him about my hard labor!" I fussed.

"I'm sorry, but it didn't look like he wanted to hear that."

"I don't give a fuck! You should've told him!"

"Look lady, I'm sorry you and that man ain't working out. But I'll be damn if I let you take your problems out on me. I've been at this job for almost ten years, and I never had anybody talk to me like this. If your disrespect has anything to do with why he ain't claiming your baby, I totally understand," she said.

"Bitch I will have your fuckin' job!"

"You ain't got that kind of power and call me a bitch again! I dare you!"

I didn't say anything, but I sure wanted to say something. She didn't even do what I asked her to do. The lady walked out of the room fussing and left me there alone with my baby. I called my mom because she asked me to call her once I had the baby. Of course, she was out of town as usual. My mom had met a man online and he lived out of state. So, she was never home when I needed her the most because she kept running behind that damn man.

Once I hung up with her, I called Bailey. She had been acting real funny with me since that shit happened with Priscilla. I figured once the baby was born, we could go back to being best friends again.

"Hello," she answered sounding uninterested.

"Hey Bailey. I had my baby!"

"Oh, congratulations!"

"Are you gonna come see us?" I asked, trying to remain hopeful.

"I don't think so Kiki."

"What? Why?"

"I don't think you're a good friend Kiki. You definitely weren't a good friend to Priscilla but pretended to be her bestie for years. I refuse to stick around until you decide to stick the knife in my back too."

"What are you saying? Because I've been a very good friend to you Bailey!" I said as tears started to fall.

Why was she doing this to me? I may not have been a good friend to Priscilla. I could admit that. However, I had been friends with Bailey a lot longer than her and I had been good to her.

"You're a good friend when it's convenient for you. Where were you when my grandmother died last year? Where were you when I had my miscarriage?"

"I-I-I-I..."

"Exactly! This thing with Priscilla and Bishop was the last straw for me. If you could do her like that, you could do the same thing to me. Congratulations on your son, but our friendship is done!"

"Bailey..."

CLICK!

"BAILEY!!" I yelled as the tears began to fall heavily. I was glad my baby wasn't in here because if he was, I know my screams would've woken him up.

The nurses had taken him to the nursery to get him cleaned and get his shots taken. No one wanted to be there for me... not Priscilla, not Bishop, not my mom or Bailey. Realizing how alone I really was in this world on one of the most important days of my life hurt like hell. How could this shit be happening? I wondered if I called Jason if he would come. But what good would that do when I wanted Bishop here? What if I called Jason and Bishop showed up to visit? Now, I'd really be fucked!

I knew he had gotten with a new bitch who was a nurse. I wished I could've delivered at the hospital she worked at. But I had to come to West Houston because that was where my doctor was. Nothing was working out for me.

Thank God my baby was healthy.

Chapter thirteen

Alissa

Things between me and Malik had been going very well. We were still going strong after three months... and it hadn't been easy. His baby mama found out about us and showed up at his house one night. She had dropped Riley off at her mom's and made her way to Malik's house to confront us. I was shocked. It was almost as if she was still carrying a torch for him. I remember that night like it was yesterday because that was the night I wanted to kick her ass.

Malik and I were sitting in the living room cuddled on the sofa watching television when the doorbell rang. Malik got up to answer the door and it wasn't long before I heard yelling. I got up to go see what the commotion was about and as soon as I rounded the corner, she was all in my face.

"This the bitch you been seeing and having around my daughter!" Priscilla barked.

Malik rushed in between us and said, "Aye, watch ya fuckin' step! First of all, you weren't invited her or inside my fuckin' house. Second of all, who I fuck with or date, don't have shit to do with you! What the fuck? You think I need your permission to date someone else? Did you need my permission when you was fuckin' my boy?"

"Damn! You still on that shit?"

"You still on this shit?" Malik countered.

"I don't want her around my daughter!" Priscilla countered.

"It ain't up to you!"

"I'm her mother!"

"And I'm her father!" Malik retorted. "At the end of the day, when our daughter is with me, I'm always going to look out for her. The same way I expect you to do when she's in your care."

"Oh, I take care of her just fine."

"So do I!"

I stood there watching the exchange between the two of them concerning Riley, but I never said anything. Whatever parenting issues they had was something that needed to be handled by the two of them. Riley wasn't my daughter or stepdaughter. She was the daughter of the man that I was dating.

"Look Priscilla, eventually, you're going to find someone to fuck with the long way. As long as that nigga respects his place and knows that Riley is my daughter, I'm cool. Whether you're cool with Alissa or not is totally up to you. But we ain't gonna beg yo ass to be cool with her. As long as Riley loves her, and she does, that's our only concern," Malik said as he draped his arm across my shoulder.

"Y'all think y'all slick. Trying to have a ready-made family with MY KID!!"

"I'm not trying to take your place..." I interjected.

"You could never take my place in my child's life... understand that!" Priscilla fussed as she rolled her neck.

This bitch was just too fucking much. I had enough of her and her slick ass mouth.

"Babe I'm gonna go in the living room and wait for you. This is your fight," I said as I kissed his cheek.

"Look, I don't know where you left Riley, but..."

"She's with my mom!"

"Well, maybe you should go pick her up and spend some time with her. This is my time with my lady, so you need to leave!" I heard Malik say.

"So, you're throwing me out?"

"Yes! Yes, the fuck I am! This is my house and under no circumstances are you allowed to come barging into my house without calling first! So, next time, if you pop up over here without calling first, you ain't getting in!"

"Wow! That's how you treat the mother of your child huh? But you can pop up over at my place anytime you want to," she countered.

"That's because I was still paying the mortgage on that house. But you know what?" I heard Malik open the draw in the table by the door. I wasn't sure what he was getting in there, but then I heard him say, "Here you go. Take your house key and from now on, you stay away from my house and I'll stay away from yours."

"What about the mortgage?"

"What about it?" Malik asked.

"You said you were paying on it. You're not paying on it anymore?" Priscilla asked.

"Priscilla you're a big girl, capable of paying your own bills. That house is almost paid off!"

"Then you should just go head on and pay it off then! After all, your daughter lives there!"

"I know where my child lives. I just think it's time for you to do your own damn thing."

"What the hell is that supposed to mean?"

"You're so damn ungrateful all the time. For some reason, you think because you bore a child for me that you're entitled to shit and you ain't. I give you a sufficient amount of child support every month to pay all of your bills and then some. If that ain't enough for you to pay your mortgage, maybe you should get a job!"

"Really?"

"Really! It's time for us to establish some boundaries and shit. I will mail your payments from now on. That way I ain't gotta go to your house and you ain't gotta come here. When it's my weekend, I'll pick Riley up from school on Friday afternoon and drop her to school Monday morning. Now, if you'll excuse me, I gotta get back to my lady..."

I heard him walking toward the door. She seemed to be really upset, but my guess is that she had it really good before Malik set boundaries. I was glad he did that because she was disrespectful. He shut the door and locked it before setting the alarm. Then he made his way to where I was sitting on the sofa.

When Malik sat down on the sofa next to me, I couldn't jump on him fast enough. Seeing him and hearing him handle his baby mama like that on my behalf and his made me horny as hell. I jumped in his lap and started kissing him hungrily. He stood up and carried me to the bedroom where the two of us made love all night long. Never in my life did I imagine being this happy with him.

The next evening, Malik and I were meeting my mom and sister for dinner. I wanted to introduce them to him because I wanted to invite him to our Thanksgiving dinner. Thanksgiving and Christmas were huge deals at our house. I also wanted his mom and Riley to be a part of it which was why it was so important for my mom and sister to meet and like him. We were meeting at T.G.I. Friday's in Sugar Land at six that evening.

As nervous as I was for the three of them to meet, I had no reason to be. My mom and sister loved Malik and vice versa. They couldn't stop praising him for the glow and smile on my face. By the time we left dinner that night, Malik, Riley and Big Mama were all invited to Thanksgiving dinner.

"Do you know how happy I am?" I asked Malik on the way back to his home.

"It's written all over your face babe."

"Thank you so much for coming to dinner."

"There's no place I would've rather been."

Malik's mom was so happy that I was in her son's life. She said she had liked me from the first night she met me, regardless of the circumstances. I really liked Big Mama also. She was a warm and loving woman. I could see how much she loved her son and how much he loved her. She also had a lot of love for Priscilla and Riley. I appreciated that she cared for Priscilla because she was her granddaughter's mother.

"I can't wait to get you home!" Malik said. I couldn't help but smile because I knew what he wanted. "Speaking of home... I want you to move in with me."

Now this was a new conversation. We hadn't spoken about me moving in with him since we got together. We had only been together for three and a half months. Was that enough time for us to know if we should live together?

"What?" I asked in surprise.

"I want you to move in with me."

"We never talked about this before."

"I know, but I think it's time we have this conversation. I love being with you Alissa. I love having you around. When you're not with me, I think about you all the time and I want you with me."

"I feel the same way. I love being with you."

He pulled into the driveway and then the garage. He shut the door and the engine, and we got out. Once inside the house, we continued the conversation. He took me in his arms and looked down into my face.

"I love you, bae," he said as he stared into my eyes.

"What?" I asked. He always said that he loved spending time with me, but this was the first time he ever said he loved me.

"I said I love you. I am madly and deeply in love with you."

"But we've only been together for three months," I said.

"Three and a half months. Look babe, ever since Olivia passed, me and Riley have been struggling to be happy. Since you've come back into our lives, we don't have to struggle to be happy anymore. We are happy. You have made us happy. I want you here with me all the time. If you don't feel the same way about me..."

"No, no! I care about you so much. I love you too, but I'm scared."

"Scared of what bae?"

"Scared of getting hurt."

"Don't you know by now that I'd never hurt you? As your man, my job is to protect and love you. I would never hurt you or let anyone else hurt you," he said. "You have to know that."

"I do."

"Then what's the problem babe. I have all this space in here for just me. Move in with me, so we can take this relationship to another level."

"You don't think it's too soon?"

"If it was too soon, I wouldn't be asking you."

"Okay."

"Okay?"

"Yea, okay."

He lifted me off my feet and twirled me around. Then he started kissing me and we ended up in the bedroom. The feelings that were coursing through my body as Malik pummeled inside me were enough to scream out his name. I didn't recall ever doing that shit before. So, yea, I must really be in love with this man.

Two weeks later, Malik paid off the rest of my lease on my apartment and I packed up my things and moved out. I couldn't believe things between me and Malik had progressed this fast. His baby mama had finally left us alone. I wasn't sure if she approved of our relationship or not, but I knew she had stop bothering us.

Riley was over the moon happy about me moving in with her dad. She wanted to move in with the two of us too. But we both knew her mom would never let that happen. Christmas came and went and thank God everyone got along. There were no incidents between Malik and his baby mama, thank God. 2019 promised to bring nothing but happiness and good times. The only thing that bothered us was that crazy ass Kiki. She had popped up the other day, but Malik wasn't there. I answered the door and her mouth dropped.

"Where's Bishop?" she asked as she held the carrier with the sleeping baby in it.

"Malik isn't here."

"So, if he's not here, why are you?"

"Not that it's any of your business, but I live here."

"You what?" she asked in surprise.

"I live here."

"So, Bishop moved you in, but still won't take care of his kid."

"That has nothing to do with me. That's between you and him."

"So, you don't care that your man is a deadbeat dad?"

"Malik is a wonderful dad to Riley."

"He's a horrible dad to Bryson though."

"That has nothing to do with me. I will tell him you dropped by," I said.

"You can invite me in..."

"Never!"

"Bitch!"

"You don't know shit about me, so I'd advise you not to call me out my name!"

"Or what?" she asked.

"You're lucky you're holding that baby. I don't have time for this shit!" I said as I shut the door in her face.

I watched on the Ring doorbell to see if she was going to leave. I couldn't wait to tell Malik about that bitch. I decided to call him and let him know that she was here.

A Thug's Romance for Valentine's Day

"Hey baby," he answered.

"Hey, you got a minute?"

"More than one for you babe. What's up?"

"That Kiki bitch just left here."

"What did she want?"

"She wants you to call her."

"I ain't calling that bitch!" Malik fussed.

"She came here with her baby. Talking about you aren't paying child support or nothing."

"Fuckin' right I ain't paying. That kid ain't mine and she knows it."

"How about this... how about I go to the store and buy a home DNA test kit. You can invite her over and swab the baby. Ship it off to a lab and you can get the results in 72 hours."

"Really?"

"Yes, really. That way it can eliminate all of her bullshit."

"Okay, let's do that," Malik said.

"Great! I'm gonna go to Walgreens right now. You can invite her over whenever you get back. As long as you do it when I'm here. I don't trust that bitch!"

"Shit, you ain't the only one."

"Okay babe, I'm on my way to Walgreens. I'll talk to you soon. Love you," I said.

"Love you too babe."

We ended the call and I headed to Walgreens. I parked my Jeep and went inside. I looked from aisle to aisle until I found what I was looking for. I made my way to the counter and stood in line. I paid for my item and was leaving the store when I heard a familiar voice calling my name. I rolled my eyes and tried to get to the Jeep at a faster pace. Right before I opened the door, I felt a tap on my shoulder.

"I knew you heard me calling you Alissa!" Maverick said.

"Why can't you leave me alone?" I asked. "I mean, is it so hard for you to walk by me when you see me?"

"Why do you keep avoiding me? I mean, I know I hurt you, but damn! The way you been acting makes me think you hate me."

"I ain't very fond of you, that's for sure."

"All that shit happened a while ago."

"What do you want Maverick?"

"I just wanted to apologize to you. I'm really sorry for the way you found out about my marriage," he said.

"Okay, is that it?" I asked.

"How've you been?"

"I'm great. I'm in a healthy relationship with a great guy who treats me like a queen."

"That's good. You look happy..."

"Very happy! I gotta go," I said as I slid in the driver's seat.

"I'm sorry..."

"You said that already. Take care!"

I shut the door and drove off, leaving him standing there watching me. What the hell was up with him? After all this time, what the hell did he expect me to say? His apologies were too late.

Thanks to that nigga, I probably would never enjoy another Valentine's Day again. I knew I wasn't looking forward to this Valentine's Day. Both me and Malik had horrible Valentine's Days last year, so I doubt if he was looking forward to it either. It was sad that such horrible memories plagued our minds on such a special day for lovers.

I got back to the house and parked my car in the garage. I was glad I had suggested the home DNA test. If anything, this test would be able to put Malik's mind at ease. He was adamant that the child wasn't his and I believed him. But I knew unless a test proved what we already knew that crazy girl would not stop coming around. Malik arrived home around four that afternoon and he called and invited Kiki over.

She was so excited to get the phone call from him that I could hear her joy through the phone even though it wasn't on speaker. I guess she thought I wasn't going to be here. That girl pulled into the driveway 20 minutes later. Malik went to let her in the house, and she walked in like the queen of the palace until she saw me sitting on the sofa.

"What's she doing here? I thought you invited me here to visit with our son," she said.

"I told you earlier that I live here," I said.

"Bishop what the hell is going on?"

"Well, since you keep insisting this kid is mine..."

"Because he is!" she said with a smirk.

"Right. Well, the only way I'm going to take care of him is if I know for sure he's mine."

"So, what... are you saying you want a DNA test?"

The confident smirk that was just on her face disappeared. "That's exactly what I'm saying. My girl went to the Walgreens and bought a home DNA test. All I gotta do is swab my cheek and your baby's cheek, ship the samples and in a matter of three days, we can get the results."

"Wow! You're really trying my patience with this shit Bishop! You never tested your other kids..."

"That's exactly why I'm gonna test yours. I'm not about to take care of another kid who ain't mine. So, if you want child support and all those other perks you looking to get from being the mother of my child, let's just take the test."

"Whose idea was that? Yours huh?" Kiki said as she glared at me.

"As a matter of fact, it was my idea. I mean, if your baby belongs to Malik, what's the problem?"

"I'm not taking that test!"

"Fine! Don't take it! But let me make myself clear, don't bring yo ass back to my fuckin' house ever again! Next time you bring yo ass here uninvited, I'll have yo ass locked up for trespassing!" Malik threatened.

"You are unbelievable! You never once thought to test Olivia, but you wanna test my baby! The fucking nerve!" Kiki voiced angrily as she walked to the front door with her baby.

Malik ran up on her so fast I thought he was about to knock her and her baby down.

"If I ever mention my children's names come out your mouth again, I'ma fuck you up! And you know me. You know I don't make idle threats," Malik said.

The girl didn't say shit, but I could see that fearful look in her eyes that I had seen that day at the mall. I only knew the sweet, gentle Malik. Something told me that I didn't want to know the street guy named Bishop. Even though the two people were the same person, apparently, he had two different sides to him. Thank God I knew the good side. I'd hate to see the other side and hoped I never would.

She rushed out of the door after that. I didn't know if she would stay away, but I hoped she did. "I knew that bitch's baby wasn't my kid!" Malik said as he picked me up and twirled me around.

He was so happy. When he was happy, I was happy. And that night in bed, he showed me exactly how happy he was.

Chapter fourteen

Malik
February 14, 2019

Today was a very hard day for me. Last year on this day, I lost my baby girl. I tried to do something special for Alissa, but it was so hard for me to not wallow in my grief. Big Mama called me around 11 that morning. Alissa had to work today. I had ordered some flowers to be delivered to her at work. But my mom called at 11 to see how I was feeling.

"Hey mom."

"Baby how are you doing? I know today is a hard day for you," she said.

"Very hard mom."

"What are you doing?"

"Lying in bed..."

"Crying huh? You sound like you've been crying."

"A little."

"Is Alissa at work?"

"Yea, she went in at six."

"Well, I'm coming over to your house."

"Aww mom, I don't feel like going anywhere..."

"Hush! This is not up for debate. I'm coming to get you, so be ready!"

"Okay," I said.

I knew better than to argue with my mom. I would argue with her and in the end, she would still win. Instead of arguing, I slid out of the bed and went to get dressed. Soon after I was done getting dressed, my mom pulled into the driveway. I grabbed my phone, wallet and keys and walked out to meet her. I slid into the passenger's seat and leaned over to kiss my mom on the cheek.

"You aren't looking too good honey. Today is Valentine's Day," my mom said.

"I know what day it is mom."

"Look, I understand last Valentine's Day was a hard one for you..."

"You think?" I asked sarcastically.

"Don't get snippy with me son! You ain't too old that I can't bust you in the mouth for being disrespectful!" My mom was right, and I didn't mean to snap at her like that.

But she was acting like Valentine's Day was a great day with good memories and shit. It wasn't. Last Valentine's Day I lost one of the loves of my life. My baby girl was gone and she wasn't coming back... ever!

"I'm sorry Big Mama. This is just a really hard day for me," I said as we pulled into the parking lot of a flower shop. "What are we doing here?"

"Come on in there with me. You'll see," she said with a smile.

She got out of the car and I followed her inside the flower shop. She walked up to the counter and said she was her to pick up an order. The woman disappeared to the back and returned a short time later. She was carrying a bouquet of flowers in pink and white with a pink bear that had Olivia's name on the front. I broke down right there in the damn flower shop, not caring who was watching me.

My mom wrapped her arms around me and held me tightly while whispering in my ear.

"I know this is a hard day for you baby. That's why I'm here for you. I knew you were going to be wallowing in sorrow all day, but I'm not going to let you do that."

She released me and I dried my eyes. I paid for my mom's purchase and a pink stuffed elephant before walking out the door. I knew we were headed to the cemetery where my precious little girl was buried. As much as I didn't want to go there today of all days, I knew I needed to do this. We got in my mom's 2019 Mercedes GLA that I bought for her for Christmas and she drove us.

Once we got there, I took a deep breath before I exited the car. Carrying the elephant and flowers, my mom and I headed to Olivia's little grave. Her headstone read her birthdate and the date she died, February 14, 2018. It had her name, Olivia Jenae Rivers with the caption, 'Our Littlest Angel'. As soon as I saw it, I started crying again. My mom put her arm around my waist because I stood over her. She wasn't as short as Alissa though.

"Olivia, I'm sorry that daddy didn't protect you that night. If I could trade places with you that night, I would have done it. You deserve to be here. You deserve to be alive and happy with your sister. I love and miss you so much, baby girl. Even though you're gone, you'll never be forgotten," I said as tears streamed from my eyes like a raging river.

"It's okay to grieve baby. I know it's hard. I don't know what it feels like to lose a child, but I know how broken up I was when your Paw Paw died. So, if you're feeling anything like how I was feeling, you will survive this. Olivia wouldn't want you doing anything less but living your life. At the end of the day, she's in a better place because she's in God's hands."

"How can she be in a better place mom? She was only two years old! She had her whole life ahead of her!"

"Sometimes, God makes decisions that we don't understand. We're all on borrowed time son. You, me, Priscilla, Alissa and Riley. Tomorrow isn't promised for any of us because at any given time, God could call us home. We have to make the most of our lives while we're still alive and breathing. You have a beautiful daughter and a beautiful woman in your life. Let them be your valentines and make it special," Big Mama said.

"So, I'm just supposed to forget my baby was killed on this same day last year?"

"Of course, that's not what I'm saying. What I'm saying is this is a very special day that you should spend pampering or catering to your lady. I just don't want this day to go by and you not acknowledge it. She told me about her horrible Valentine's Day last year, but she also said it was a good day. You wanna know why?"

"Why?"

"Because she said that was the day she met you and the night she met Riley," my mom informed me.

"She told you that?"

"Yea. She said she knew today was going to be hard for you, but she was going to be there for you. She's a good woman son. I love Priscilla but she wasn't the one for you. Alissa is."

"You really believe that mom?"

"I do, but the question is, do you believe it?"

"I've had strong feelings for her since the day we met when we bumped into each other at H.E.B. Of course, it took us a while to get together, but I feel that she's the one too."

"Then do something special for her to show her that. Olivia would want you to be happy."

"I know mom. I just wish I could trade places with her..."

"Don't ever say that! God chose that baby for a reason! You must never question that reason."

We placed the items we bought for Olivia and picked up the old flowers to toss.

We said our prayers for her and left. When I walked away from her grave, I no longer felt that strain on my heart the way I felt when we walked into the cemetery. It felt like my heart was singing. Even though Olivia was gone, and I'd never forget the tragic way she died, I couldn't stop living because of it. I hadn't really planned anything for Alissa tonight. I was going to give her some dick and call it a night.

But as my mom pointed out, Alissa was special... she was the one. She deserved more than just some dick. She deserved it all.

"Ma you really like Alissa, don't you?" I asked once we were on our way.

"I love Alissa. You know that she calls to check on me every other day?"

"I didn't know that."

"Well, she does. I've also been spending time with Shirley, her mom."

"Really? What do y'all fine chicks be doing?"

"We go to the salon to get our hair done, to the nail shop, the mall, or just enjoy lunch somewhere. Alissa's whole family is a blessing and I thank you for finding that young woman. She's good for you," she said.

"She's great for me!" I corrected.

"She really is. That's why you should do something special for her tonight."

"I definitely will ma." I leaned over and kissed her on the cheek. "Thanks ma."

"For what?"

"For restoring my faith in V Day."

"You're welcome baby," she said with a huge smile. "I just want you to be happy."

"I am!"

"And it shows."

She pulled up to my house and I gave her a big hug. "I love you ma."

"I love you more baby."

I hopped out of her car, a man on mission. I checked the time and it was almost one o'clock. I had to go to the trap house before I started shopping for Alissa. I wanted to make this day really special for her. I hopped in my truck and headed to the trap. Since Alissa had moved in with me, I had been neglecting my street duties. But I trusted Keys with everything, so I wasn't worried about nothing.

When I arrived, business was running smoothly as usual. I knew I could trust Keys to do the job I paid him handsomely to do. I knocked the secret knock on the door and was let in.

"S'up nigga?" I greeted Keys with a brotherly hug.

"Wassup with you? I didn't think you were coming by today," Keys said.

"Yea, well, I had plans to lay up in bed all day crying, but you know Big Mama. She wasn't about to let that shit happen. She came over and picked me up. We just came from visiting Olivia."

"How did that go? How do you feel?" Keys asked.

"I feel great! You know Big Mama has a way of pointing things out to make you see things differently than before."

"Yea, I love Big Mama!"

"So, where Tony at?" I asked.

Keys bent his head low like he didn't want to talk about it.

"Uh, I let that nigga go."

"What? Why?"

"That nigga was stealing from us bro!"

"Wait a minute. Tony Shivers was stealing? The dude we took in like a brother and gave work to was stealing?" I asked. I was totally surprised.

"Fuckin' right! I caught that nigga red-handed. I had called to talk to you about it, but I knew this wasn't going to be a good day for you, so I hung up. I didn't wanna burden you," Keys said.

"When the hell did that shit happen?"

"This morning. I walked in and that nigga was stuffing his pockets..."

"And you just fired him? You getting soft nigga?"

"I ain't getting soft. That nigga is outta there," he said as he slid his finger across his neck.

"Damn! I had no idea that nigga was on some shit like that!"

"Well, I got some other news for you bro."

"News like what?"

"That nigga been sleeping witcho baby mama," Keys said.

"I had a feeling..."

"What? You knew?"

"I wasn't sure, but I suspected. I caught that nigga coming out her house one day and when she came to the door, all she had on was a robe. I figured something was going on between them two..."

"And you still let that nigga work for you? Hell, if he had fucked with Tamika, he wouldn't have made it out of that damn yard!" Keys said.

"At the end of the day, Priscilla ain't my woman no mo. If she wanted to fuck with that nigga, that was on her!"

"Bishop, did you know yo baby mama was pregnant by that nigga?"

"What? Nooooo!"

"Yea, that's probably why he was stealing and shit! He said he just found out that she was pregnant and knew once you found out, you would stop paying her mortgage or some shit like that!"

"I stopped paying that shit two months ago! She's too fuckin' disrespectful and ungrateful!" I said. "Now she's pregnant!"

"For a deceased nigga!" Keys smirked.

"Lawd! Aye, that's on her," I said as I raised my hands in the air.

"Well, lemme get yo shit bro. I'ma be right back," Keys said as he went to the back room. I couldn't believe all the shit he had just told me.

They had to murk Tony cuz he was stealing from me to provide for my baby mama cuz she got pregnant by him. The whole scenario had my head spinning. This was some crazy shit. Keys walked back to the front carrying two duffle bags. He looked like he was straining, so I went to help him.

"Damn this shit heavy! Whatchu put in there... bricks?" I asked with a laugh.

"Na nigga. You just ain't been here in a while!"

"Gotdamn! You gon' have to come out and help me with that shit!"

"Ain't said but a word bro."

We each carried a bag out to my truck and stashed it in the secret compartment in the floorboard. Then I gave Keys dap and hopped in the truck.

"Give my baby a kiss for me. Tell her unc will be by to see her soon!" Keys said.

"I'll let her know."

That nigga and I had been through so much shit. As long as we had each other, business would always be good. He was the most loyal friend I had, and I trusted him with my life. That was why he was the godfather to Riley. I left and headed back to my side of town. I wasn't sure what I was going to get Alissa for Valentine's Day, but after speaking with my mom, I had a much clearer head. I knew exactly what to get her.

I placed a call to Yolanda Barker. She was a chef who had catered for me a few times and tonight I needed her. She said she had a prior engagement, but she could whip up something for me and have it delivered to my house by six. I told her that would be great. I stopped by the florist to order some flowers to be delivered to my house at six. Then I went to my friend Joe to pick up something special for my lady.

I knew she was going to be tired after a long day, but what kind of man would I be if I didn't plan something special for her? She deserved everything I had planned and then some. I made it home at 4:40, so that didn't leave me with much time to get things done. I hopped in the shower and washed all of the day's remnants off my body.

I hopped out of the shower and got dressed. At a quarter to six, the doorbell rang. I went to open it. It was the flower shop delivery. I had ordered 20 dozen of red roses and had the delivery guys place them everywhere in the house. I wanted them to be the first things Alissa saw when she walked in. I tipped the dudes and they left as the catered food was arriving.

The young girl walked in and removed the trays from her heated bag. "Miss Yolanda said as long as you keep them in the oven on 250 degrees until you're ready to eat, they should be good."

"What did she cook?"

She handed me a menu and placed another container on the counter. "You have to keep the cheesecake in the fridge."

"Thank you," I said with a smile.

"Oh, she also sent this as an apology because she couldn't come here." She reached in the bag and handed me a bottle of wine.

"She is something else. I'm gonna have to call her tomorrow," I said. "Here you go."

I handed her a hundred-dollar bill for her tip and her mouth dropped to the floor. "Oh my God! This is the biggest tip I've ever gotten!" she gushed. "Thank you so much!"

"You're welcome." I escorted her to the door. "Enjoy the rest of your evening."

"Thank you. You too!"

Before I shut the door, I saw my lady pulling into the driveway. She pulled into the garage and I shut and locked the door. I grabbed a single rose from one of the crystal vases and was standing by the door when she entered.

"Happy Valentine's Day baby!" I greeted as I handed her the rose. I hugged her tight and kissed her soft lips.

"What's all this?!" she asked in surprise. As she walked around and saw all the roses, tears formed in her eyes. "You did all this for me?"

"Hell yea! You're my baby and I wanted tonight to be special for you."

"Aw, baby!"

She wrapped her arms around my waist, and I lowered my head to kiss her again.

"Thank you so much!" she said as she rested her hands over her heart. "You even wore a suit. You look so handsome!"

"Hugo Boss just for you baby!"

"Can I get cleaned up? I won't be long," she said.

"Go ahead. I'll be right here waiting for you."

She rushed to the bedroom all happy. That smile that she had on her face was what I wanted to see. I planned on keeping it there for as long as God allowed me to. While she was taking a shower, I set the food on the dining room table. When I heard her coming out of the bedroom, I lit the candles.

"Alexa, play *There Goes My Baby*!"

"Playing *There Goes My Baby* by Charlie Wilson," Alexa responded as the music played while she walked out.

She looked beautiful in the black dress that I had purchased for her. She came into my arms and I held her close. Tonight was going to be special...

Chapter fifteen

Alissa

Knowing everything that happened on Valentine's Day last year, I wasn't looking for anything special this V Day. I figured I'd give my man some kitty and rock him to sleep. He had sent me a beautiful bouquet of flowers at work. I appreciated that he did that for me since I didn't think we'd be celebrating this day at all. I hadn't been feeling well, but I had patients to tend to until six o'clock this evening. Whatever I was feeling was just going to have to be put on hold because my patients came first.

After my shift was over, I headed home not expecting anything special. I expected this day to be hard for Malik, harder than it was for me. All I wanted was to hold him tight and listen if he wanted to talk about his feelings. However, I did have a surprise for him though. I wasn't sure if he was going to be excited or not, but I could only hope.

When I pulled into my driveway, I saw a white van parked in the driveway. He was standing in the doorway talking to some chick. That wasn't even what caught my

A Thug's Romance for Valentine's Day

eye though. What caught my eye was the fact that he was wearing a suit... a burgundy suit with a black shirt and a burgundy and black striped tie. My man looked good, really good.

Shit, we may have to go straight to the bedroom looking as fine as he's looking.

I walked into the house to be greeted by him holding a rose. Flowers were everywhere and I could smell a delicious aroma coming from the oven. My man also smelled good enough to eat. My heart was racing because never had any man done something so special for me. Tears immediately sprang to my eyes as he kissed me. I couldn't believe he did all that for me.

I excused myself to take a shower. Walked into the master bedroom and he had a black dress on the bed for me. On top of the dress was a diamond necklace. "Well damn!"

I quickly jumped in the shower filled with excitement. Once I was finished getting ready, I headed back out to meet my man. He had already put the food on the table and lit the candles. When I heard, *There Goes My Baby*, I couldn't help but feel special. He hugged me tight before pulling out my chair. The food looked delicious.

It was filet mignon with shrimps in a wine sauce drizzled over it. There was also some mashed potatoes with gravy and green beans. It looked amazing. As we ate and discussed the days events, he told me Big Mama had taken him to the cemetery to visit Olivia. He said they had a long talk about his future and me. That meant a lot to me that his mother liked me so much.

"Do you know my mom told me that you're the one?" Malik asked as he smiled at me.

"She did?"

"Yes. She told me that you're the one for me and I better hold on to you."

"Well, she's a very wise woman."

"She is, which is why I'm gonna take her advice." I watched as he reached in his pocket, stood up then knelt before me.

"What are you doing Malik?" I asked even though I had an idea.

"Baby I love you so much. One year ago, we met and it changed my life forever. You are the woman that I wanna spend the rest of my life with, so if you'll have me, I wanna make you my wife. Will you marry me Alissa?" He opened the box to reveal a stunning diamond ring. I had never seen a ring so beautiful or so big.

"Yes!" I said as he slipped the ring on my finger.

I grabbed both sides of his face and kissed his lips. I couldn't believe how lucky I was to have a man like

Malik Rivers in my life. If someone had told me that a year after getting my heart broken by Maverick, I'd be getting proposed to, I don't think I would've believed them. Yet here we are!

"I have something for you too." I got up and went to my bag on the counter. I pulled out the small red and white bag with the hearts on them and handed it to him.

He placed his hand in the bag and pulled the paper out. As he read it, I could see the smile forming on his face. He looked at me and asked, "You're pregnant?"

I nodded my head.

"Aw, baby!" He lifted me up off my feet and kissed me deeply.

He carried me to the bedroom where we made love all night long. I couldn't believe that this wonderful man was all mine. I couldn't wait to share the news with my family, Big Mama and especially Riley. This was the absolute best Valentine's Day ever!

Well, at least that was what I thought...

A novel by Lady Lissa

Epilogue

Valentine's Day 2020
Kiki

Man, this was some bullshit! Life should not be this damn hard. I was supposed to be living in a big ass house while raising my son. I was supposed to be driving a nice ass car instead of my 2015 Honda Civic. What the hell made Bishop ask for a paternity test anyway? He took care of Olivia without a fucking question. She wasn't his either, but he still was there. But couldn't do the same for me and mine. That was some bogus shit!

Jason and I were now living together, and he was helping me raise my son. We lived in an apartment on the northeast side of town. I guess I should be happy that my baby daddy had stepped up huh? Aht! He wasn't even the one I wanted. I wanted Bishop. Bishop had the big money, big house, fancy cars. I guess I just gotta be grateful for what I did have, especially since I didn't bother telling Jason about Bryson until Bishop asked for that DNA test. That was when I knew my lie wasn't gonna fly.

A Thug's Romance for Valentine's Day

Today was Valentine's Day and Bishop's wedding day. I started to crash the party but changed my mind. If he wanted to marry that little lollipop kid, let him do it. I tried to repair my relationship with Priscilla and Bailey, but those bitches were mad mad. They still wanted nothing to do with me. It was cool. I'd just find me some new friends. Fuck Valentine's Day!

Knowing my man, he'd probably come in with some damn carnations because roses were too expensive... ol' penny pinching ass!

Priscilla

Today was a hard day for me because it was Bishop's wedding day. I didn't really want to be there, but since Riley was the miniature bride, I felt that I had to be. I had given birth to Tony's son five and a half months ago but couldn't find that nigga anywhere. I didn't know if he ran out on me or what. One day he was here and the next day he was gone. I hated that shit. I was already struggling because Malik didn't wanna pay my mortgage anymore. Yea, he gave me money every month, but I had things to do for myself too.

He expected me to spend the money on just bills to provide for Riley, but what about me? I had weave that needed to be sewn in, nails that needed to be glued on and clothes I needed to buy. Not to mention I wanted a new car, a Mercedes GT. I mean, he got Big Mama a new whip so why he couldn't get me one. I wasn't his Big Mama, but I was to his daughter.

I couldn't believe he was actually marrying that girl. Like what the hell did she have that I didn't? The last thing I wanted to do was go there and pretend to be happy for them, but sometimes in life, we had to put our personal feelings aside for our children. I loved Riley very much, so of course I was going to do this for her.

I'd be lying if I said I didn't wake up thinking about my precious baby Olivia. I missed her little butt so much. I hated that they chose the day I lost my daughter to get married. That was so insensitive of them. As I looked at myself in the mirror, I smiled at my reflection. I knew I looked good as fuck. Maybe Bishop would see how good I looked in my tight red dress and want to marry me instead. I knew that was just wishful thinking though.

Malik

The day was finally here. The day that I would make Alissa my wife. I was excited and a bundle of nerves at the same damn time. It was hard to believe that two years ago was the worst Valentine's Day ever, and now this one is the best one ever. Alissa gave birth to my daughter three months ago, so there was a lot that needed to be done to get us to this point. She had her dress fitting only a month ago. She couldn't do it before because of the pregnancy. Our little girl looked exactly like her mother, beautiful.

As I stood at the altar watching my Riley walk down the aisle with her pretty white dress, she looked so happy. She held her bouquet of flowers and smiled so bright. Big Mama sat holding the baby and looking every bit the angel she was in her lavender gown. Just because it was Valentine's Day didn't mean we had to be dressed in red and white, right?

I saw Priscilla and her friend Bailey in attendance. Thank God she let that bullshit bitch Kiki go. That wasn't her real friend anyway. I didn't think Priscilla was going to come though. She was pretty upset because we chose this day to tie the knot. She thought we were being disrespectful to Olivia's memory, but I didn't think so. And I didn't think Olivia would think so either. Of course, Priscilla was entitled to her own opinion. We didn't have to care about how she felt.

As everyone stood to welcome the bride, the singer began to sing, *Always and Forever* by Heatwave. When I laid eyes on Alissa, my eyes instantly became watery. Seeing my bride look as beautiful as she was made my heart swell with joy. Her mom escorted her down the aisle as they walked hand in hand. Keys rubbed my shoulder and handed me a hankie.

Thank God for that nigga. Otherwise, I would've been looking like that nigga on *The Best Man*. Now, I was far from a punk, but I couldn't help but cry as I stared at my beautiful wife to be. When she finally made it to the altar, we held hands.

"You look amazing!" I said.

"So do you babe. You ready to get married?"

"You have no idea how ready I am," I said.

So, the ceremony commenced. I couldn't be happier if I had won a million dollars in the lottery. Marrying Alissa, my best friend, was better than anything I could've asked for. I truly believe God made her especially for me. She was the Ying to my Yang and the vows I would speak to her today would guarantee that. My mom was right when she said Alissa was the one because she was. She was the one for me, for my daughter, and for our daughter.

Alissa

Today was the day. Nothing was going to ruin it for us. Not even finding out that Maverick had died of cancer three weeks ago. I guess that was why it was so important for him to apologize to me and make sure that I forgave him. I kind of felt bad that I hadn't told him that I forgave him, but I did. If I hadn't forgiven him, I would've never been able to open my heart to love Malik.

I didn't think we'd be able to pull this wedding off three months after I gave birth to Khloe, yet here we were. I had six bridesmaids and my sister was my maid of honor. The colors were lavender, silver and pink. I wanted the pink to be in memory of Olivia. As I stared at myself in my princess ballgown that my mom insisted was fitting for the occasion, I had to admit that she was right. Shelby put the tiara on my head and my veil.

"Oh my God! You look incredible!" Shelby said.

The tears in my mom's eyes let me know that she thought the same thing. "You like it mommy?"

"I love it baby! You look beautiful!" my mom gushed.

As the music began to play, my sister turned to me and asked, "Are you ready?"

"Oh yes ma'am," I said with a huge smile.

"You look beautiful Lissa!" Riley said. "You look like a princess!"

"Thank you, baby. You look like a little princess too!" I said.

"Yea, my dress is just like yours!"

"It sure is. Are you ready for me to marry your daddy?" I asked.

"Yea! I'm ready for you to be my new mommy too!"

That melted my heart when she said that. "Then let's get this show on the road," I said.

Everyone filed down the hallway which led to the ballroom where our wedding was being held. The double doors opened and me and my mom began our walk. The look on Malik's face when he laid eyes on me was priceless. I prayed that the photographer captured it. He had tears in his eyes as I walked to the altar.

When it was time for our vows to be said, I didn't need any paper because I knew exactly what I wanted to say. I just spoke from my heart.

"Malik, when we first met, I gave you a pretty hard time. I never imagined that we'd be standing here today in front of our family and friends pledging our love for one another. You came into my life and literally swept me off my feet. When you first told me that you loved me, I thought I had imagined hearing it. I thought I was the only one feeling that way. Hearing you tell me that restored my faith in love. Being loved by you has been the greatest feeling. We have a beautiful daughter together and I have a beautiful stepdaughter. Thank you for making all my dreams come true. I promise from this day forward to always give you the best of me. I promise to never take you for granted. I promise to love, honor and cherish you forever."

"Malik, you may recite your vows."

"Shit, I don't know if I can top that, but let me try. Alissa, the circumstances which we met weren't the greatest. But during that time, it showed me what a caring and compassionate woman you are. The lengths you went through to make me and my little girl feel loved means the world to me. Losing Olivia had me feeling like I didn't do a good job as a father. But you came along and helped me to see that accidents happen. I now have a renewed faith in love, fatherhood and the future. With you by my side, we can conquer the world. You're my real rider baby. I never in a million years would've thought myself worthy enough of your love, but you loved me anyway. You accepted me with my flaws and all and never made me feel anything but loved. Today I am marrying my best friend and the only wife I will ever love. Thank you for making all my dreams come true. I promise from this day forward to always give you the best of me. I promise to never take you for granted. I promise to love, honor and cherish you forever," he concluded.

After Malik finished his vows, there wasn't a dry eye in the house. I turned to Riley and asked her to come up to the altar. She smiled happily and practically bounced her little way over to where we stood. I bent down to her level and looked her in the eyes as I held her little hands.

"Riley, I am not only marrying your daddy today, but you too."

"Me too?" she said in confusion.

"Yes baby. I just want you to know that I'm going to be the best step-mommy you could ever have. I'm going to love you, cherish you and be there for you always. I have something for you," I said as I reached in the little white satin bag I held on my wrist.

I pulled the tiny ring I got for her out of the bag and put it on her little finger.

"It's beautiful Lissa! Thank you!" Riley squealed as she wrapped her arms around my neck.

Today was the happiest day of my life. I married my best friend in the whole world. This just proved to me that you should never give up on love. There was someone for everyone out there and Malik was for me!

The end!!